THE SEVENTH VIRGIN

When Constable Joe Bentley rescues what he thinks is a nude woman from the freezing waters of the River Thames, his catch turns out to be an exquisitely modelled tailor's dummy stuffed with thousands of pounds' worth of bank notes. Later that same morning, the dead body of a man is found further downriver. Superintendent Budd of Scotland Yard, under pressure to prevent millions of counterfeit notes from entering general circulation, must discover the connection between the incidents, and stop a cold-blooded murderer on a killing spree.

GERALD VERNER
AND CHRIS VERNER

THE
SEVENTH
VIRGIN

Complete and Unabridged

LINFORD
Leicester

First published in Great Britain

First Linford Edition
published 2019

Novelisation by Chris Verner, based on an
original scenario and characters created
by Gerald Verner

*A catalogue record for this book is available
from the British Library.*

ISBN 978–1–4448–4081–0

Published by
F. A. Thorpe (Publishing)
Anstey, Leicestershire

Set by Words & Graphics Ltd.
Anstey, Leicestershire
Printed and bound in Great Britain by
T. J. International Ltd., Padstow, Cornwall

This book is printed on acid-free paper

1

It was late February, just before dawn. The River Thames lay under a blanket of fog, muffling the noises of the city that managed to break through like a discordant and ghostly symphony. The wind had freshened with the turn of the tide, driving the fog in swirls and eddies around the Thames River Police Duty Boat 'Thames D7' as it passed the Houses of Parliament, a looming mass on the port side, and headed at five knots towards Westminster Bridge.

Constable Mike Larkin, steersman and engineer, shivered at the helm. He was tall and thin, with dark hair, hollow eyes and prominent cheekbones, making him appear older than his thirty-one years. He wore a pencil-thin black moustache. 'It's perishin' cold,' he moaned to his friend, Constable Joe Bentley.

Joe Bentley, of medium height, well built, and possessing rugged good looks, clapped his hands together in an attempt to warm them up. He was two years younger than Larkin. 'A couple of hours still to go.' He nodded in agreement.

'Time for a cuppa,' suggested Larkin meaningfully.

The third member of the crew, Sergeant Proctor, portly and middle-aged, went to a locker and returned with a thermos flask which he handed to Bentley.

'All I can think of is hot coffee with bacon and eggs in the warm canteen,' Bentley said as he took the thermos from his sergeant. Unscrewing the top, he poured his friend a mug full of steaming tea.

'Not me,' retorted Larkin, accepting the mug of tea from Bentley gratefully and taking a sip. 'I'm off home for my breakfast.'

'You're lucky to have a wife waiting to cook for you,' Bentley said enviously. 'Try living on your own.'

'I have tried it, Joe — that's why I got married. If you'll take my advice, you'll find yourself a nice woman and settle down before you get too old.' Larkin nudged Bentley in the ribs. 'What about Glenda Lane? She's all right, isn't she? You'd better be quick, mind, or she'll be snapped up.'

Bentley looked at his partner's gaunt face, illuminated by the low cabin light and a red ignition indicator from the control panel. 'I see enough of cops all day and night. I don't want to end up with a WPC.'

'That doesn't fool me,' said Mike Larkin with a grin. 'I've seen the way you look at her.'

Bentley shook his head in denial. 'Must be your imagination.'

'I don't think so,' Larkin persisted knowingly. 'You'll end up a lonely old man if you don't get a move on.'

'You know her father's a copper, don't you?' Bentley confided, picking up his sergeant's mug.

'What's that?' Larkin turned to him with interest.

'He's a detective inspector,' answered Bentley conspiratorially.

'She never mentioned that to me,'

grumbled Larkin, as if he should have known.

'He's at Scotland Yard,' Bentley continued, pouring hot tea into the mug. 'He works undercover. Maybe that's why she doesn't talk about him much. Did you know her mother was killed in the blitz?'

'That's tough,' said Larkin, sipping his tea gratefully. 'Does she live with her dad?'

'When he's at home, which I gather isn't often, because he's usually on an assignment.'

'Do you know where she lives?'

'She lives in Stepney.'

'She's a nice gal, Joe,' Larkin said warmly as he steered the duty boat towards the stone arches of London Bridge.

Bentley frowned as if this fact hadn't occurred to him before. 'Yes, she is.'

Larkin grinned at his friend. 'For someone who doesn't want to end up with a WPC, you seem to know an awful lot about her. I'm sure she could do with a shoulder to cry on.'

'It's starting to get light,' observed

Sergeant Proctor as Bentley handed him his mug of tea.

A watery sun was attempting to break through the patchy fog as they passed under London Bridge, heading for the Pool of London. As Sergeant Proctor took the empty thermos back to the locker at the stern, a bulky shape loomed out of the fog on their starboard side.

'Joe, look out!' warned Bentley, bracing himself.

Larkin dropped his mug of tea as he saw the dark mass was upon them and took evasive action. He wrenched the wheel, steering the boat to port in an attempt to avoid the danger.

But he was too late!

The rusting sides of a drifting Thames lighter crashed into the duty boat with a high-pitched screech, ripping off the fendering as its steel hull scraped along the starboard side. As the duty boat swung hard to port, tipping low in the water, Proctor, who was just approaching the locker, was caught off balance. With a cry, he stumbled heavily into the side.

'What in hell's name?' cried Larkin,

trying in vain to avoid another collision with the threatening barge.

Proctor held on to the gunwale of the launch, but it was wet and slippery with the damp fog and he slipped sideways, righting himself by gripping onto a cleat.

'Look out!' yelled Bentley as the hull loomed close, towering over them.

There was another crash and a splintering of wood as the lighter collided into them again.

This time Proctor lost his balance completely. Before he could get a grip, he was flung overboard. Flailing his arms and legs, he landed with a splash and was immersed in the swirling waters of the river.

'Man overboard!' yelled Bentley, looking over the side for any sign of his sergeant, but the boat had moved on and the fog closed in around it.

'What?' cried Larkin, startled, peering through the windscreen in an attempt to locate the barge. He didn't think he'd heard right.

'The sergeant!' Bentley yelled in warning, his eyes huge. 'He's fallen in,

Mike. Quick, we've got to turn back and find him or he'll be a goner in this current.'

Larkin slammed the gears into reverse. The engine throbbed as Larkin took it to maximum power. The boat bucked like some angry beast as the propeller churned the waters and slowed them down.

Bentley switched on the searchlight, and the beam caught the looming hull of the barge as it slid eerily past.

Larkin steered the boat hard around in a tight circle while Bentley directed the searchlight on the choppy surface of the water, looking for Sergeant Proctor.

'Any sign of him?' Larkin asked.

'I can't see anything! This perishing fog — he can't be far.'

'Have we gone back far enough?'

'It's hard to tell, isn't it?' said Bentley as a wave of panic surge through him. 'He's got be here somewhere.'

Sergeant Proctor, desperate to keep himself afloat, saw the stern of the duty boat disappear into the fog. He realised he was in a very precarious position, in danger of drowning if he didn't get out of the freezing water. Something wet and slimy rubbed against his cheek and he vigorously swam to avoid it. Then it happened again, and he realised it was a length of rope. He managed to get a grip on it with one hand, and corkscrewing round quickly, grabbed at it with the other. Immediately he felt himself dragged through the water. Hand over hand, he pulled himself along the rough rope, which was a good two inches thick. He realised the rope must be trailing behind the drifting barge and tied off at the stern, and he might use it to climb clear of the water . . .

The police duty boat passed him on his port side, its searchlight missing him completely.

'Help!' Proctor yelled several times. He could feel his body was about to shut down with the cold — if he could only pull himself up . . .

'Did you hear that?' Bentley shouted, straining to listen. 'I'm sure I heard something.'

'I heard it, but it's hard to tell from

which direction,' Larkin answered.

'I could swear that cry came from in front of us. Mike, we've gone too far downstream.'

'It's difficult to judge,' said Larkin. 'We're moving with the current.'

They could now hear faint cries coming out of the fog.

'That must be Proctor!' exclaimed Larkin. 'How did he get back there?'

'Never mind; take her around. That has to be the sergeant. Head towards him.'

Sergeant Proctor kept up his cries for help, hoping the crew of the duty boat would hear him and come in pursuit. Winding his legs around the rope to get a tighter grip, he pulled for all he was worth and managed to haul his body free of the swirling waters. Getting a purchase on the lighter was another thing altogether. It was high in the water, indicating it wasn't carrying a load. The steel lighters had no means of propulsion and were basically long hulls that could be filled with coal or other merchandise, and several could be pulled by a tug. The sergeant had dealt with lighters all his working life on the river. The hull was welded to a steel deck, leaving nothing he could grab hold of; and he knew, as he hung clear of the water, he wouldn't be able to get on board. He kept crying out, hoping he could conserve enough strength to cling onto the wet and slippery rope until help arrived.

'Thames D7 to TDH — come in please,' Bentley spoke into the hand-held microphone, calling their headquarters at Wapping.

'TDH to Thames D7 — TDH to Thames D7 — over, what is your position?' the man in the operations room at Wapping replied.

'Between London Bridge and Tower Bridge,' Bentley answered. 'Proceeding down river towards St. Katherine's Docks — speed approximately five knots — over. Patrol boat D7 in collision with drifting lighter — Sergeant Proctor overboard — over. Need help with rescue. Some damage to patrol boat — over and out.'

'I can't see any sign of him,' Bentley said, switching off the microphone and scouring the surface for signs of Proctor.

The fog was clearing a little, and the watery sun was trying to break through. Ahead, Larkin could just make out the drifting barge. 'Aim that light on the barge, Joe,' he instructed. 'I think I can see something moving.'

'It's the sarge,' said Bentley, peering into the fog. 'He's hanging on to a stern rope.' Grabbing the loudhailer, he began yelling, 'Sergeant Proctor — ? Sergeant Proctor — ?'

'Keep that damned light on him,' said Larkin, steering towards the barge. He could just make out 'LTC 34' in white letters on the stern.

Suddenly there was a terrific crash from up ahead, and sounds of splintering wood, followed by a cry that was cut short.

'What was that?' shouted Larkin, straining to hear more.

'I can't see,' answered Bentley, as the sun was obscured by a patch of fog. 'That barge collided with something.'

'Proctor's not there anymore!' Larkin cried, peering through the windscreen. 'He's fallen off the rope with the impact.'

He swept the searchlight across the water near the stern of the barge and managed to pick up the sergeant in the water.

'Keep that spot on him,' instructed Bentley eagerly.

Leaning over the side, Bentley watched the sergeant drawing closer. He grabbed a lifebelt attached to a length of rope tied off to a cleat and threw it with all his strength towards Proctor, who swam towards it and clung on. Bentley grabbed the lifebelt with a long boathook and pulled Proctor towards the stern of the boat. He managed to get a good grip on his sergeant's arm and was able to heave him aboard.

'Are you all right, Sarge?'

'Of course I'm not all right!' gasped Proctor irritably. 'I'm frozen through and soaking wet. How can I possibly be all right?'

'I meant are you wounded?' Bentley answered, looking worried, wrapping him in a blanket.

'Only my pride, Joe,' answered the sergeant through chattering teeth. 'That Thames lighter smashed into something.

I felt it — didn't you hear it?'

'I heard a helluva crash,' Bentley answered, opening a box containing an oxygen cylinder and a face mask.

'The impact threw me off,' said Proctor. 'We'd better try and find out what happened.'

'First, I'm going to give you a bit of oxygen, Sarge,' Bentley warned, gently placing the mask over his sergeant's nose while cracking open the valve. 'You look all in.'

Mike Larkin grimaced. 'Tide's on the flow. It'll carry that drifter downstream towards Wapping. I'm going in pursuit.'

He was increasing their speed to overtake the Thames lighter when the searchlight picked out floating debris in the water and what looked like the upturned hull of a small boat.

'Looks like the barge collided with another boat,' Larkin commented. 'Written it off.'

'What's a small boat doing on the river at this time of the morning?' Bentley asked, leaving Proctor breathing oxygen while he switched on the microphone.

'Thames D7 to TDH — come in please, over.'

'TDH to Thames D7 — TDH to Thames D7 — what is your position? — over.'

'Downstream of St. Katherine's Docks,' answered Bentley. 'We think a Thames barge 'LTC 34' has collided with a smaller vessel and sunk it — looking for survivors — need help with rescue. Sergeant Proctor back safe on board — over and out.'

Bentley peered over the side. 'No sign of anyone.'

'Keep looking,' Sergeant Proctor instructed, handing Bentley the oxygen mask. 'There can't be two vessels adrift — someone was most likely rowing that other boat.'

'Yes, Sarge,' agreed Bentley excitedly. 'I can see something over on our starboard side, tangled up in the floating wreckage. Look there! Can you see it, Mike?'

'Yes, I see it,' Larkin said grimly. 'Get that spot on it.'

'Looks like a body,' said Bentley, aiming the spotlight. The beam rested for a moment on platinum-blonde hair fanning out on the surface. Then it was gone.

Larkin put the gears into reverse to slow down. 'Looked like a woman,' he said in a tense voice.

'I thought so,' Bentley agreed grimly, playing the searchlight over the churning water in an attempt to catch another glimpse of the platinum-blonde hair.

Larkin swung the wheel. 'I'm moving in close; keep your eyes skinned.'

Bentley peered into the murky water. 'Dead slow, Mike,' he instructed. 'I think the current might have taken her under.'

Suddenly the body rose to the surface, and Bentley was able to reach out towards it, straining to get a grip on a bare arm, but the body drifted away from him.

'I nearly got her then. Slow down, Mike, and keep to starboard,' he instructed, his voice strained with the exertion of leaning over the side and reaching out towards the floating woman. 'No clothes on. Nude.'

'Any sign of life?' Larkin asked anxiously.

'Not that I could detect. She's floating face down. Looks bad,' Bentley grunted as the platinum-blonde hair came almost within his reach. 'Easy now — reverse . . . '

Bentley stretched out again and managed to grip an arm. 'Got her!' he exclaimed triumphantly, and then he knew at once something was wrong. 'This isn't real,' he said in disappointment, heaving at the arm. 'It's a dummy — a damned heavy one.'

He held on to the mannequin with one hand while grabbing a coil of rope with the other. He managed to thread the rope under the arms.

'It's one those shop window dummies. They can't be as heavy as this.'

He heaved on the rope and managed to lift the mannequin onto the gunwale, where he balanced it for a moment to get his breath back. Then, exerting all his strength, he heaved it onto the deck.

'Will you look at that!' exclaimed Larkin. 'All made up and everything!'

16

Bentley stood staring at the mannequin that now lay in a twisted position on the deck of the boat. The platinum-blonde hair was wet and matted. The blue eyes with their long dark lashes caught the cabin light and appeared to be staring at him.

'I've never seen a shop window dummy as lifelike as that,' he said uneasily. 'She's creepy.'

Larkin laughed, 'Just suit you, Joe, and a lot cheaper to run than Glenda!'

Another searchlight was coming towards them. It was Duty Boat 'Thames D4'.

'The cavalry at last,' Proctor said with relief. 'About time.'

Larkin increased his speed to take them back to Wapping.

'This is one of the strangest things we've ever encountered,' Bentley commented. 'Why would a boat be crossing the Thames at this time of the morning in freezing fog with a shop window dummy on board?'

'Beats me,' agreed Larkin.

Joe Bentley looked at the mannequin

17

and thought for a moment. 'A thing like that . . . what's it value?'

Larkin shrugged. He had no idea and was too cold to care. 'Whatever it is, it's not worth the risk of rowing across the Thames in the dark. I wouldn't hold out much hope for whoever was in that boat.'

'So why do it?' Bentley persisted.

Sergeant Proctor indicated the other duty boat. 'If they can fish someone out alive, maybe we'll find out.'

2

WPC Glenda Lane was awakened by her alarm clock at six-thirty, like any other day — except this day wasn't going to be like any other. But she didn't know that as she slipped out of bed and turned on the gas tap by the fire. She waited for the gas to hiss through and, lighting it with a match, dived back beneath the warm covers to wait while the ceramic pillars grew red hot, taking the chill out of the air of her freezing bedroom. When the room had warmed up, she slipped out of bed to begin her routine of washing and dressing, which began with emptying her hot water bottle and hanging it on the hook on the back of the door and ended with the application of a little make-up and a self-critical examination in a full-length mirror. She saw a slim woman of twenty-five, of medium height, with bright hazel eyes set in a pleasant rounded face crowned by straw-coloured hair cut in a short style.

Drawing the curtains, she looked out upon a row of nondescript houses. The view, softened by fog, did nothing to dispel the monotony she imagined the day would bring. She had a quick brain that demanded constant stimulation. From the age of eighteen, she had been taught to drive various classes of vehicle as part of the war effort; and she had to admit to herself that despite the constant threat, life had been more active and interesting in those days than it was now.

She heaved a sigh as she turned off the gas fire, lifted her jacket off its hanger, and carried it downstairs to prepare her customary meagre breakfast. Her father had been staying in a room in Whitechapel while working on an undercover investigation, so she was on her own. She brewed a small pot of tea, put two slices of bread under the grill, and waited for them to turn brown. Buttering the toast, she washed it down with a cup of tea. Putting on her coat and grabbing her shoulder bag, she set off for the bus stop, waving a cheery good morning to those she met. Everyone in the street knew Glenda.

Even when the fog lifted, Wapping High Street remained in deep shadow from the wharfs that loomed above her. She walked briskly past Wapping Old Stairs, which led down to the lapping waters of the river; past the historic Town of Ramsgate pub snuggling beside Oliver's Wharf; and along by the waterside gardens and Aberdeen Wharf. She entered the headquarters of the Thames River Police, older than the Metropolitan Police Force, of which they now formed a division, by thirty years. She was proud to be a part of the world's first organised police force formed in 1798, to tackle theft and looting from ships anchored in the Pool of London, the stretch of the River Thames from London Bridge to just below Tower Bridge. Their motto was 'Primus Omnium'.

Seated at three rows of desks in the high-ceilinged hall that served as the operations room, men and women operated the communications network that kept the Thames River Police in touch with their duty boats out on the river.

Glenda would have much rather been out on the river in a duty boat, where emergencies could occur at any time and often did, than sitting at a wooden desk for most of the day in the operations room. It was a routine she had quickly adapted to but was now growing tired of; it wasn't what she wanted to do with her life. Moments of excitement relieved her daily routine, but there were few of them and they usually involved other people. She wondered what the day might offer to brighten her mood, and was pleasantly intrigued when she heard about the dawn adventures of those aboard Thames D7. Everyone had been talking about the 'rescue' of the mannequin.

'You've had a busy morning,' she greeted enviously as Mike Larkin and Joe Bentley burst into the operations room.

'Busier than you might think,' replied Bentley, carrying a mug of hot coffee from the canteen for her. He put it down on her desk.

'Oh, thank you Joe,' Glenda said with a

warm smile. 'That's really thoughtful of you.'

Larkin winked at Bentley.

'There's been a new development,' Bentley told her eagerly. 'We've just recovered ten thousand pounds! Well, nearly ten thousand.'

Glenda did a double take and stared at Bentley in astonishment. 'That's a fortune. Where did you find it?'

'When we took that dummy to the evidence room.'

'We couldn't believe how heavy it was,' said Mike Larkin.

'When we lifted the dummy onto the table,' continued Bentley, 'the head turned towards me!'

'No!' Glenda's eyes opened in amazement. 'That's creepy!'

'She *is* creepy,' Larkin agreed.

'It was just the way the side of her face touched the top,' Bentley explained. 'There's a join in the neck; you can hardly see it.'

'What did you do?' Glenda asked, fascinated.

'I grabbed her head and swivelled it,

pulling at the same time. It came right off!'

Glenda's eyes opened even wider.

'The dummy is made of some sort of hard plaster material and it's hollow inside,' added Larkin.

'There's a two-inch collar that fits into the neck,' Bentley continued. 'Something made me look inside, and I noticed a packet wrapped in oilskin paper. I pulled it out and then saw another one. There were five of them altogether.'

'The packets were full of fivers, two thousand pounds in each one,' Larkin explained. 'Ten thousand quid!'

'Was the money real?' Glenda asked suspiciously, taking a sip of her coffee.

'It looked real,' said Larkin. 'Real enough to buy us all a drink!'

Glenda looked at them reprovingly. 'You haven't.'

'Of course not,' said Bentley with a grin. 'Tempted though — one packet had been opened and there were a few notes missing.'

This was just the sort of excitement Glenda craved and wished she could be more involved with. She was envious of Bentley and Larkin's life on the river and sometimes wished she had been born a man. 'How do you suppose it got there?' she inquired.

Bentley had been wondering the same thing. 'Stolen from a bank, I expect.'

Glenda screwed up her nose. 'But why was it inside a mannequin — that's what they call them, isn't it?'

Bentley nodded. 'I suppose 'dummy' is a bit of a rude name to call such a beautiful woman.'

'Do I detect a touch of jealousy, Glenda?' Larkin joked.

Glenda laughed and flushed red.

'When I'd got all the packets out, I put her head back on,' finished Bentley, running his fingers through his unruly hair.

'That was kind. I'm sure she appreciated that, Joe,' Glenda said with a grin.

He was enjoying the opportunity to chat with her and laughed. 'It seemed the decent thing to do.'

'I suppose these notes could be forgeries,' Glenda suggested, her brows drawing together in a small frown.

'They don't look like forgeries,' Bentley responded. 'They're crisp and shiny and printed on proper bank paper. If they're counterfeit, I reckon they're damned good.'

'That's enough money to set me up for life,' murmured Glenda with a wistful smile. 'I could buy a house and everything I wanted.'

'That's why crooks are crooks, Glenda,' Bentley pointed out. 'They look for a short cut to fortune.'

'Any news about Sergeant Proctor, Glenda?' asked Larkin.

'He's gone straight to the hospital to get pumped out,' she answered. 'That water's lethal if you swallow any of it — all that sewage floating about, it's disgusting. First time he's fallen in, isn't it?'

Larkin nodded. 'It's also the first time we've argued with a thirty-ton drifter,' he said with a grim expression. 'I don't recommend it. We need to find out where that barge came from.'

'Your boat is out of commission for a

few days while it goes in for repair,' she warned them with a worried look. 'It's badly scraped along the starboard side. Telford wasn't too pleased about that.'

'I bet he wasn't, but there wasn't a lot we could do about it. Thames lighters don't normally come loose,' Larkin explained, referring to the barge by its proper name. 'I hope he's not looking to blame us for the damage. In that fog we couldn't see it coming.'

'The ropes get damp and this cold weather freezes 'em up. The lightermen can't undo the knots so they cut them with axes. I've seen it happen,' said Bentley. 'Doesn't happen often, but a barge can get away.'

Glenda looked at her notes. 'LTC 34, you said?'

Bentley nodded. 'That's what was written on the stern.'

'We're checking the registrations,' said Glenda, looking up. 'We'll contact the owners.'

'I'd better ring home,' said Mike Larkin, thinking of his wife preparing his breakfast. He needed to tell her he wouldn't be home for a while, not until he'd made a full statement to Superintendent Ramsay. He walked over to an empty position and picked up the telephone. He turned to Glenda. 'Is the super in yet?'

'On his way,' she said. 'He wants you two to stay put 'til Telford's grilled you. I'll need to be sending a basic report through to the information room at the Yard. Did you make a note of the serial numbers on those banknotes?'

Bentley took out his notebook and, turning to the current page, put it in front of her.

'Those are the numbers,' he said. 'They run consecutively.'

'Thanks.' She smiled at him and began copying them down. 'No doubt we'll be hearing back from the Yard if there's been a bank robbery involving new notes — they'll have the serial numbers, and with any luck we'll get a match.'

'It could mean this morning's events are part of something much bigger,' Bentley said, smiling enthusiastically. Like

Glenda, he was eager to be part of something greater than the usual day-to-day routine.

'Bit of luck you finding the mannequin,' she replied. 'It could have sunk, couldn't it?'

'You're dead right,' Bentley agreed. 'A few minutes more and she'd have gone under. Mind you, the packets with the notes were well sealed. I don't reckon they would have got damaged, waterlogged or anything. She'd have probably drifted upstream and washed up somewhere at low tide.'

'I expect you thought you were rescuing a damsel in distress,' Glenda said mischievously. 'It must have been a huge disappointment when all you got hold of was a shop dummy!'

'Mannequin, Glenda!' corrected Bentley with a wink. 'We mustn't let her hear us calling her a dummy.'

Glenda raised her eyebrows. 'So she's a bit of a looker.'

Bentley nodded, grinning. 'She's the goods all right. Expensive to make, I should think. All that detail — much

more lifelike than your average mannequin.'

'He's fallen for her,' Larkin teased. 'It's
very worrying. Expect to see them out on
the town anytime soon!'

'I'd rather find a shop dummy than a
dead woman,' Bentley replied with a
wintry smile. 'Is there any news on the
rower of that boat that got smashed up?'

Their banter subsided and was
replaced by concern that their colleagues
hadn't managed to rescue or recover the
body of whoever had been rowing the
boat before it got hit by the drifting
barge.

'D4 and D9 are still searching the area,'
she told them. 'Nothing on that yet, but
they've secured the barge.'

'Maybe more dummies will turn up,'
Larkin remarked.

'If there are more, they haven't found
them,' reported Glenda. 'Probably sunk
by now.'

Bentley scratched his head. 'It's the
queerest thing when you stop to think
about it — all that cash inside a
mannequin.'

Glenda stopped copying the serial numbers from Bentley's notebook and finished her coffee. 'You've no proof your woman came from that boat, have you?'

Bentley chewed over the odds. 'Let me put it this way, Glenda. It was a coincidence that boat was hit by a drifter at that time of the morning. It was in the wrong place at the wrong time, and that's very bad luck for anyone in it. But it would be an even greater coincidence if she hadn't been a passenger on that boat and landed in the water some other way at around that time. She must have fallen in shortly before I fished her out. Any longer in the water and she'd have gone under.'

'I agree with Joe,' Larkin said, puzzling over the incident. 'There is no 'other way'. I'm pretty certain she was on that boat right up to the moment of impact. Someone was rowing it to the opposite shore.'

Glenda looked puzzled. 'At that time of the morning?'

Bentley shrugged his shoulders and raised his eyebrows. 'It suggests to me the rower had some sort of rendezvous — maybe planned to hand over the cash.'

Glenda wrinkled her nose. 'Why struggle with a heavy plaster dummy on a boat? Why not take the cash out of the dummy and put it in a bag? That would make much more sense.'

Larkin nodded. 'She's got a point,' he agreed.

Bentley looked at both of them fatalistically. 'Whatever the reason, unless the rower was a very strong swimmer, there's a floater out there somewhere.'

The telephone on Glenda's desk rang and she picked up the receiver. 'WPC Lane,' she answered. 'Yes, sir, I'll tell them to come up.' She glanced at the two constables. 'That was Telford. The super's arrived and wants to see you two in the evidence room right away.'

★ ★ ★

Resting on a long wooden examination table in the evidence room was the platinum-blonde mannequin. Next to it were five stacks of five-pound notes and a pile of oilskin wrappings. Superintendent Ramsay was looking at the notes thoughtfully. He was a big man with thinning wavy hair and weather-beaten features from a lifetime on the river.

'Morning, Larkin. Morning, Bentley,' he boomed as the two constables entered the evidence room. 'I hear you've had quite a night — an argument with a lighter, Sergeant Proctor overboard, and a dramatic rescue.'

'Sorry for the damage to the boat, sir,' Bentley apologised. 'The fog was bad and we never saw that barge coming.'

'We'll have a serious word with the owners of that lighter,' Ramsay growled. 'It shouldn't have happened.'

Detective-Inspector Telford entered. He was as thin as a rake, with angular features, and eyes like a hawk.

'Interesting catch,' he commented, indicating the mannequin. 'Other debris taken from the river, oars and broken pieces of the wrecked boat, are being assembled out in the yard, piece by piece as they're brought in. It's a standard waterman's boat. Unfortunately there's no sign of any rower yet.'

He spoke to Bentley and Larkin. 'You can both make a written statement upstairs in a moment, but first would you tell us in your own words what happened? Ten thousand pounds is a lot of money. We want to know where it came from and where it was going.' He looked enquiringly from one to the other, his eyes resting upon Bentley. 'Bentley, you fished her out of the water. Why don't you kick off.'

Both the constables went through their experiences of two hours ago, from the moment they collided with the Thames lighter to the retrieval of the female mannequin. When they had finished, Telford commended them for saving Sergeant Proctor.

'We might learn something from the serial numbers,' Superintendent Ramsay commented, indicating the stack of banknotes. 'Superintendent Robert Budd will be coming down from the Yard and an expert from the Bank of England will be meeting him here. He's a chap named Frobisher. They're keen to take a look at this lot. What do you think about these notes, Telford? They look real to me.'

Telford picked up one of the banknotes and examined it carefully. 'If they're forgeries, they're good ones — they'd fool most people.'

Glenda Lane entered the room with a grim expression on her face. 'A report's just come in over the radio telephone from Duty Boat D4, sir,' she announced, addressing the superintendent. 'They've pulled the body of a man out of the river just beyond Shad Thames.'

'Drowned?' Ramsey asked.

Glenda nodded, 'I'm afraid so, sir.'

'Any details?' Telford enquired.

Lane glanced at her notepad. 'Man in his forties, five foot eight, short dark hair, receding. They're bringing him in now. There hasn't been time to make a complete examination, sir.'

'Of course not,' said Telford. 'At least we've found him.'

Ramsay grunted an acknowledgement. 'We need to find out who he was and everything else about him without delay.'

'I'll get onto it right away,' Telford

acknowledged, crossing over to a telephone.

Ramsay glanced at Glenda Lane, who was staring with fascination at the lifelike mannequin. 'That will be all, Lane. Thank you.'

She was focussing on the mannequin's left foot. 'Do you mind if I take a look at something, sir?' she asked him, stepping forward without waiting for a reply. She lifted the mannequin's foot and examined the sole closely, angling it to the light as she wiped away a bit of river slime with her finger. 'There are markings here,' she pointed out. 'See that — V 7?'

Superintendent Ramsay came closer to get a better look. 'Ah, yes, you're quite right, Lane. It's some kind of identification mark, probably the model type, V7. Might help to trace the thing,' he said with a wry smile. 'The Seventh Virgin.'

Telford put down the receiver and came over to take a look.

'Better follow that up without delay too,' Ramsay instructed. 'Sharp of you to spot that, Lane.'

Glenda couldn't prevent a quick smile

of satisfaction crossing her face. 'Thank you, sir.'

'Telephone those markings through to the Yard,' Telford ordered. 'Keep them up to date with everything.'

'Right away, sir,' Glenda confirmed, making for the door.

'I've a feeling this is part of a much bigger picture,' said Ramsay, turning to Larkin and Bentley. 'It's been a long night, but these are exceptional circumstances, and I'd like you to stay until the super gets here from Scotland Yard and this Frobisher chap arrives. They're bound to have questions. You can complete written statements in the canteen. I'll arrange for Lane to call you when you're required.'

3

Colonel Blair, Assistant Commissioner for the Criminal Investigation Department at Scotland Yard, put down the report he had been reading, smoothed his neat grey hair, and leaned back in his chair with a worried frown.

With a brief knock at the door, Superintendent Robert Budd lumbered into the room, uncertain whether the information he had to impart would improve the assistant commissioner's bleak mood.

'Sit down, Budd,' said Colonel Blair, brandishing the report. 'Something has to be done about this. The Bank of England and the home secretary are not very pleased with us, and you can understand why.'

The big man took the report with a podgy hand and squeezed his huge bulk into a chair, which protested with creaks and groans. He looked sleepily through the columns of figures in the report that provided amounts, dates, and geographical information.

When he had assimilated the report, Mr. Budd looked up and faced the assistant commissioner uncomfortably. He'd been watching the totals build up over the past few months as the banks pulled in quantities of counterfeit notes, only able to identify them by their bogus serial numbers because the fakes were so realistic.

'You can see from these latest figures there's a considerable amount of counterfeit money turning up in the system, race tracks, and casinos — anyplace this slush can be laundered for real cash. And that's only what has been detected,' Colonel Blair continued.

'Of course, once we know the fake serial numbers, we can spot others by 'em,' Mr. Budd remarked sleepily. 'If that collector chap — '

'Reginald Aitken,' snapped the assistant commissioner.

Mr. Budd opened his eyes wide at the harsh interruption. 'That's right, sir. If

Mr. Aitken hadn't spotted one and sounded the alarm, it's doubtful we would have known much was going on.'

Colonel Blair nodded and frowned. 'One fact is certain, Budd — the total handed in to date is a drop in the ocean compared to what's still out there in the system. That's not very gratifying.'

Mr. Budd scratched his chins as he considered carefully how to reply, mindful that anything he did say could be used against him. 'Frobisher agrees these notes are exceptional quality — very hard to detect,' he said.

Colonel Blair twiddled a pencil between his fingers irritably. 'The river police found ten thousand pounds concealed inside a mannequin this morning. What do you make of this latest development? Is it connected?'

Mr. Budd shifted his weight uncomfortably in the creaky chair. He strongly disliked reporting to the assistant commissioner when he was in the middle of an investigation, particularly as he hadn't managed to marshal enough facts to draw any useful conclusions based on firm evidence.

'I'll be one step further to answerin' that question when I go to Wapping and show 'em to Frobisher, who's on his way over there from the Bank of England,' he said in his sleepy drawling voice. 'At this moment, we don't know for certain the incident at Wapping is connected with the counterfeit operation. Frobisher will examine the notes and then we'll know fer certain if the cash is real or counterfeit. I was about to go over there ter meet him when you asked me to come up here.'

Colonel Blair didn't much appreciate being gently reminded he was responsible for slowing down the investigation by taking up his superintendent's time.

'Answer me this, Budd. Why would a man row across the Thames in the dark with a dummy full of banknotes?' He tapped his pencil impatiently on the blotter. 'Who was this man, and why didn't he take the money out of the dummy and put it in a canvas bag? That's what any sensible person would have done — far less trouble and less noticeable than running around with a platinum blonde in a boat.'

Mr. Budd's hand subconsciously crept to his waistcoat pocket, where he kept his black cigars. Realising where he was, he resisted his temptation and reluctantly withdrew it. He opened his eyes, pursing his lips.

'As I understand it, sir, a chain of events were set off early this mornin' due to one of them big coal barges, a Thames lighter they're called, which had broken loose from its moorings. It drifted on the tide downstream towards Tower Bridge and collided with a boat, destroying it at about five-thirty this mornin'. I think we can assume the dummy was aboard that boat and entered the water at the moment of impact. If it hadn't been for a duty boat at the scene, the dummy would have sunk. At approximately eight-thirty this morning, another duty boat found a drowned man in the river who is yet to be identified. He hadn't been in the water very long, and I would find it very surprisin' if he wasn't the rower of that boat.'

Blair shifted uneasily in his chair.

'As you are aware,' added the big man hastily, 'for several weeks now I've had a detective inspector working undercover. He's recently discovered this counterfeit money is coming into the Port of London from abroad, and from his latest report I'm confident he's close to a breakthrough.'

'You think that ties in with this money found in the mannequin?' asked Blair, making a brief note on his pad.

The big man closed his eyes. If the assistant commissioner hadn't known him better, he might have assumed he'd nodded off to sleep.

'If it ties in, this could be the break we've been waiting for,' he answered evasively.

'I sincerely hope so,' Colonel Blair acknowledged. 'I have the utmost confidence in your abilities, Budd. I know you'll put a stop to this counterfeit gang in the end — sooner rather than later, eh?'

Mr. Budd returned to his office to pick up his hat, annoyed his meeting with the assistant commissioner had delayed him. He found the melancholy Sergeant Leek waiting to see him.

'Mr. Frobisher has arrived in Wapping,' the sergeant announced gloomily.

Mr. Budd took one of his black cigars from his pocket and with great enjoyment proceeded to light it. 'Order me a car. I need to get over there straightaway,' he grunted.

Leek's long face brightened up at the prospect of escaping the office. 'I've always liked the river,' he said.

'Then it's a pity you won't be seein' it,' answered his superior unkindly, blowing out a cloud of acrid smoke. 'We need to trace this mannequin. Did you arrange for a photographer?'

'Yes, Bradshaw's available,' Leek answered, referring to his notebook. 'Oh yes, Wapping have found a mark on the sole of one of the dummy's feet.'

'Well, what is it?' snapped the stout superintendent.

'Only a mark — V7.'

'That could be very important. I want you to find out where you can get hold of the most expensive shop window mannequin, platinum-blonde hair, eyes, eyelashes, make-up — the most realistic imitation of a real woman.'

'Do you want me to get hold of one?' the sergeant asked, looking puzzled.

The big man slowly shook his head. 'You'll 'ave to find your pleasures some other way,' he said sarcastically. 'I don't want to buy one. I want to know the chain of supply from manufacturer to shop. I'm interested in any distinguishin' marks, in particular any that match that V7.'

The lugubrious Leek sighed. 'This isn't going to be easy.'

'Investigatin' isn't supposed to be easy,' retorted Mr. Budd, giving Leek a withering look.

'Where do you think I should start?'

'Contact some of the big stores — find out where top-quality dummies come from. There's most likely a distributor somewhere who supplies 'em all. Get an address, but don't make any contact because we don't want to frighten 'em off. As soon as you've got anything useful, contact me immediately.'

'Anything else you want me to do?' asked Leek miserably.

'As a matter of fact, there is. Draw up a list of London banks capable of large-scale money laundering.'

'How am I supposed to know which banks are capable of that?'

'Investigate,' Mr. Budd advised.

★ ★ ★

When Mr. Budd arrived at Thames Division at Wapping, he spoke briefly to Superintendent Ramsay to introduce himself; and then, accompanied by Detective Inspector Telford and the police photographer Bradshaw, he went straight to the evidence room.

Frobisher was already busy carrying out a preliminary comparison of the banknotes found in the mannequin with a control selection he had brought with him, with the aid of a large magnifying glass.

Telford handed Mr. Budd a file of statements from those involved in the morning's events and sent for Mike Larkin and Joe Bentley. When they saw the lethargic-looking superintendent, they thought he was the exact opposite of how a detective ought to be. The stout man wedged himself in a chair and wearily asked them to repeat their experiences on the river earlier that morning. At one point they thought he had dropped off to sleep, not realising he was listening attentively, his brain never more active.

'Do yer have any reason to believe this shop dummy didn't come from the boat that collided with the barge?' he asked, yawning.

Both constables repeated their earlier discussion with Glenda Lane. They couldn't prove the mannequin was on the boat because they hadn't *seen* it on the boat, but they thought the chances it had entered the river from anywhere else most unlikely.

'If she'd been in the water for any length of time, she'd have sunk, sir,' reiterated Bentley. 'It was lucky we were on the spot.'

The big man heaved himself out of his

chair and lumbered over to the evidence table. He examined the dummy, whose head was turned at an angle towards him — the platinum-blonde hair drying out, the lifelike blue eyes with their long lashes beseeching him to find the culprit that had brought her to such an ignominious end. It would have been easy in a different light to believe for a few moments that she was real. He wondered how many more mannequins might exist somewhere stuffed with banknotes.

'The head comes off?' he asked Bradley, who promptly demonstrated how to remove it by turning and tugging it.

Mr. Budd noticed the part that fitted into the neck of the torso was well greased. He ran his eye down her legs until he came to the markings on the sole of her left foot and tilted his head to one side in order to examine the V7 code closely. He called Bradshaw over.

'Bradshaw, get some close-up shots of this mannequin,' he ordered, and then pointed to the left foot. 'And those marks in particular.'

While Bradshaw began setting up his

apparatus, Mr. Budd turned his attention to Frobisher.

'Mornin' Frobisher,' he greeted. 'Thank you for comin' over at short notice to look at these fivers. Are they fakes?'

'I have no doubt these banknotes are from the same source as the others, Superintendent,' he confirmed. 'They're forgeries.'

'We might be onto somethin' at last,' Mr. Budd grunted.

'Indeed, this is a significant discovery. I would say very significant,' agreed Frobisher as he slipped his magnifying glass into a soft pouch and stowed it away in a battered leather case. 'Like the few we've already taken out of circulation, these are premium quality. They're printed on real bank paper, which is watermarked. I've just ascertained it's the same watermark as the others — but incorrect. It's not a British watermark; it belongs to some foreign currency. I think it may be Italian.'

Mr. Budd stroked his chin. 'Interestin'. How many people handlin' these notes would look at the watermark and notice that?'

'Very few. It's unlikely the average bank clerk would know how the real watermark should look. They wouldn't notice unless they were expressly looking, and had the presence of mind to compare these with an example of the real thing. That's precisely why these counterfeit notes are getting into the system so easily without being detected.'

'Could these have originated from wartime plates?'

Frobisher shook his head emphatically. He pointed to a signature at the bottom of one of the five-pound notes. 'Notice the chief cashier. They're signed Percival Beale. Beale took over from Kenneth Peppiatt in 1949. These have been forged since 1949, and that makes them current.'

Mr. Budd stroked his chin. 'If these forgeries are printed on what appears to be real banknote paper, with a watermark, we can surely identify where the paper came from.'

'You think this paper was manufactured in order to print a genuine foreign currency, and a quantity of it was stolen?'

'That's exactly what I think. If the watermark could be identified as being Italian, for example, it's reasonable to assume the paper originated in Italy. It might provide us with a lead.'

Frobisher chewed this idea over for a moment. 'Identification by that method is certainly a possibility.'

'The fact that the plates are recent doesn't mean the paper is,' the superintendent pointed out.

'Of course it doesn't. I'll look into that right away.'

'Then there's the serial numbers,' the detective continued sleepily, picking up a wad of notes and slowly shuffling through them.

'Like the recent forgeries we've managed to apprehend, these printed sheets have been through a numbering machine. The serial numbers are consecutive, but invented,' replied the bank official. 'They don't exist in official records.'

'Unusual to have consecutive serial numbers on slush, isn't it?' He felt the paper between a thumb and forefinger. It was crisp and silky, and would have fooled him.

'The consecutive serial numbers have provided us with an effective way to trace the notes,' Frobisher said. 'By filling in the gaps in the sequence, we can predict which notes are still in circulation. It's a staggering number, proving we're up against a very sophisticated operation. The print quality is excellent, which almost certainly means these notes have been produced on a superior screen printing machine. As you've rightly pointed out, it would be very hard for any forgers to get this type of paper in this country. It's very tightly regulated.'

'Someone, or several people, got hold of this paper, engraved the plates, acquired the right kind of printin' press and built up an efficient means of distribution,' Mr. Budd said thoughtfully. 'That takes knowledge and clever organisation. If we can track down just one aspect of this operation, it could open up leads to the whole of it.'

'Oh, most certainly. I'll look into this watermark right away. We'll see if we can come up with something.'

'Derek Lane is convinced these banknotes have been smuggled in from abroad,' the superintendent confided.

'In view of the paper and what's happened this morning, I must agree with him. I think it's more than likely the origins are European.'

Mr. Budd scratched the back of his head. 'One of the reasons I requested Derek Lane to assist with the investigation was because he'd worked for the security services during the war and helped uncover a plan of the Germans. You worked with him on Operation Bernard, didn't you, Frobisher?'

'The best counterfeit banknotes ever produced,' Frobisher said with admiration. 'With the exception of this lot, which in my opinion are just as good, if not better.'

'Forcing concentration camp prisoners, selected for their expertise, to forge British five-pound notes in order to destabilise the British economy strikes me as a similar kind of thing to what we 'ave 'ere,' suggested Mr. Budd, thoughtfully.

'It's on a smaller scale for now, but it won't be for long if we don't put a stop to it. There may be a connection.'

Frobisher considered this idea for a moment before giving his opinion. 'I can't think what it would be. The German forgeries from Sachsenhausen were completely different to these new plates.'

'Those who worked on the counterfeit plates at Sachsenhausen would have had a good apprenticeship, wouldn't they?' persisted Mr. Budd. 'It is not inconceivable that one of 'em is working on this little caper. That could explain why forged notes might have been smuggled into England as part of a foreign operation.'

Frobisher selected a crisp banknote from the stack and held it up. 'I'd like to take ten of these with me, as samples.'

'That will be all right, sir, as long you sign a release form,' Telford intervened, crossing to a telephone and ringing through to WPC Lane. 'Bring a release form to the evidence room for ten of the counterfeit banknotes straightaway, Lane. It's for Mr. Frobisher from the Bank of England. Make it snappy, I don't want to keep him waiting.' He looked over at Frobisher and caught his eye. 'The release form will be here in a moment, sir.'

'These recent events on the river, Telford,' Mr. Budd began, 'suggest we may need to look for a cargo boat coming to the docks from Europe bringing in mannequins like this one. Customs might know something.'

'We'll get onto customs right away, sir,' promised Telford.

'This funny money might not only be hidden in mannequins,' warned the superintendent. 'You might look for any other means by which large quantities of notes could be slipped by customs.'

He wandered over to the evidence table and stared contemplatively at a pile of clothes, a pair of worn shoes, and other assorted objects.

'Did these things belong to the dead man?' he asked.

'They did, sir,' Telford confirmed.

Mr. Budd examined the items. There was a steel watch that was made in Russia, an empty wallet with the contents drying out beside it, two ten-shilling notes, some loose change, a bunch of keys, and an unusual pocket knife with a bone handle that was well worn. He picked up the knife, still wet from the river. As he waved it at Telford, a few drops of water flew off and landed on the polished floor.

'There's a small shop off New Fetter Lane specialising in knives,' he informed the detective inspector. 'You may know of it. It might be useful to get someone to take this knife over there and find out if anyone recognises the type. They may be able to tell us where it originated. I've a feeling it could help us.'

Glenda Lane entered the room briskly and approached Telford. 'They'll be here in an hour to take the body to the morgue for post-mortem,' she informed him quietly.

'I'd like see the body before it goes,' Mr. Budd requested.

'Superintendent, you mentioned Detective Inspector Lane earlier — this is his daughter, WPC Lane.'

'Nice to meet you,' replied Mr. Budd, looking at Glenda with mild curiosity. He recognised the resemblance to her father.

'Good morning, Superintendent,' greeted Glenda with a warm smile. 'I've heard my father speak of you often, sir.'

Mr. Budd grunted. 'Nothin' derogatory, I hope.'

'No sir, he has a lot of respect for you. It's a pleasure to finally meet you.' She handed a piece of paper to Telford. 'This is the release form you asked for.'

Telford took the printed form from her and handed it to Frobisher. 'Here we are, Mr. Frobisher — if you'd just sign this, we're all done.'

Telford picked up the pocket knife with the bone handle and handed it to Glenda. 'We need to find out more about this knife. Superintendent Budd tells me there's a shop off New Fetter Lane that specialises in this sort of thing. It'd be helpful to get their opinion.'

Glenda wasn't hearing him. Her face had gone white.

'Is something the matter?' asked Telford, not concealing his irritation at her lack of concentration.

She was staring at the knife in her hand

with horror. 'May I ask where you got this, sir?' she asked in a faltering voice.

Mr. Budd swung round, his usually sleepy face transformed into one astutely alert. In that one moment, he knew —

'It was one of the items we found on the body we fished out of the river this morning,' answered Telford, his brows drawing together. 'Is something wrong, Lane?'

Glenda was breathing erratically and appeared to have lost focus. Tears were forming in her eyes as she turned the knife over with her fingers.

'May I see the body, sir?' she asked, trying to remain calm.

There was no mistaking the urgency in her voice. She was in the grip of a fearful premonition — desperately clinging for support to the discipline she'd been taught.

For a moment, Telford was caught off guard. He seemed about to refuse, but her demeanour and the look of concern on Mr. Budd's face emphasised the knife had triggered something very serious.

'Follow me,' he said crisply.

Mr. Budd's mind was in turmoil as he followed the procession down a long corridor and out into the open yard and slipway, where the smells and sounds of the river assaulted his senses. The fog had lifted, exposing the watery sun that had been trying to break through a layer of thin grey cloud since dawn. A tug pulling six lighters was slowly moving down river. The superintendent produced an evil-smelling black cigar and sniffed it, but refrained from the temptation to light it and stowed it away again. Unless he was under a misconception, his investigation into the counterfeiting operation was about to take a very unpleasant turn of events.

Under a four-poster frame covered with blue tarpaulin was a large but shallow stainless steel bath, hidden from the prying eyes of those travelling on the river. Lying in the bath, covered by a flimsy shroud, was the outline of a naked body.

Telford, with a concerned glance at Glenda, lifted the corner of the sheet aside to reveal the head and shoulders of a man. Glenda gasped. She stared at the dead man's face in disbelief and horror as her worst fears were confirmed. As she saw the deep gash to the side of his head, she envisaged the steel prow of the barge cleaving into the boat. Her hands flew to her face. It was a dreadful sight to behold, and she turned away, on the verge of collapse.

Mr. Budd stepped quickly forward to support her. He also recognised the dead man.

Glenda's body slowly drooped like a wilting flower. 'That's my father,' she managed to whisper.

Mr. Budd nodded. 'I'm so very sorry,' he murmured gently.

'Undercover, always mixing with criminals.' She broke off, stifling a sob. She looked defiantly at the solemn group gathered around the body, as if they were to blame. 'This was bound to happen one day, wasn't it?'

'It can 'appen to any policeman,' Mr. Budd admitted in a low voice.

Her face looked haggard and drawn — the transformation from the smiling woman of a few minutes ago had been dramatic and ageing, as memories filled her head. Random and spontaneous, flashback after flashback from her childhood brought tears to her eyes as she was overcome with grief. She broke away from Mr. Budd, and taking out a handkerchief blew her nose.

The small group by the side of the river, huddled beneath the tarpaulin, maintained a respectful silence. They all knew how she must be feeling but could offer little in the way of consolation.

Mr. Budd, with surprising tenderness, guided the quietly sobbing woman away from the dreadful sight. He chaperoned her back into the building and took her straight to the canteen, where he ordered her a cup of strong tea.

Superintendent Ramsay marched in, as shocked as everyone else by Glenda's identification of the body. He took Mr. Budd to one side. 'I had no idea,' he said.

'Of course you didn't,' Mr. Budd replied.

Ramsay's voice was full of regret. 'I wish we could have avoided her seeing her father like that. This is a totally unexpected turn of events. That barge — what a terrible accident to have happened.'

Mr. Budd nodded in agreement. 'Detective Sergeant Lane was working undercover to track down the gang responsible for these fake banknotes. I believe he was close to a breakthrough and must have managed to get 'old of that mannequin as proof of the counter-feiter's operations. Then that barge . . . '

'Incredible bad luck,' cut in Ramsay, with a sympathetic glance at Glenda. 'I need to get her home.'

Glenda sipped her tea while staring at the floor and remembering why she had joined the police force. She was making a supreme effort to pull herself together.

Joe Bentley entered the canteen, wide-eyed at hearing the news. He felt awkward and unsure how best to handle the situation. He went up to Glenda and stood by her helplessly.

'I don't know what to say Glenda . . . this is terrible.'

She gave him a grateful smile but was

obviously embarrassed by the fuss. 'I'll be all right Joe,' she told him, sipping some more hot tea. 'Just give me a moment.'

Mr. Budd had gone to Telford's office to take a call from Sergeant Leek when he bumped into Frobisher, who was just leaving. Frobisher had heard about the identification and looked as shocked as everyone else. He'd known Derek Lane since the war.

Mr. Budd's eyes narrowed as he listened carefully to what Leek had to tell him and then spoke to Telford. 'My sergeant has discovered that mannequin is Dutch. It's manufactured by a firm in Amsterdam called Vandekkan. He tells me the mannequins are imported into this country by an outfit that call themselves Natural Art Studios. I've asked Sergeant Leek to find out all he can about them — a history of the business, who owns it, and when it was started up. But here's a very interestin' fact — they own a small showroom and warehouse in Mews Street, by St. Katherine's Docks.'

'The location certainly fits,' remarked Telford. 'It looks like our seventh virgin is a Dutch woman.'

Telford spoke to Dene Wainwright, deputy head of customs for the Pool of London, and the Dutch connection was established.

'Twenty shop mannequins were unloaded two days ago from a Dutch ship called the *Gelderland*, registered in Rotterdam,' Wainwright informed him.

'Do you have the name of the captain?' asked Telford.

'The captain's name is Issak Slaatama,' answered the customs man.

Telford relayed this information to Mr. Budd.

'Everything's pointing to this counterfeit operation being based in Holland, with distribution of the fake notes run from over here,' Mr. Budd said, relieved he had at last something concrete to report to Colonel Blair. 'Is the *Gelderland* still in port?'

Telford made a call to the Port of London Authority. After several minutes on the telephone, he had his answer.

'The *Gelderland* leaves Surrey Docks bound for Amsterdam at the turn o' the tide this evening,' he told the sleepy-eyed detective.

'I'll arrange to have it watched, and we'll see if anyone interestin' turns up,' Mr. Budd said. 'We'd better pay this Captain Slaatama a visit. Will you arrange for customs to accompany us, preferably the same men who checked in the *Gelderland* and examined the dummies?'

'I'll get onto it immediately,' Telford confirmed.

4

'We need to pay this Natural Art Studios outfit a visit, but it's important nothing alerts the counterfeiters we might be onto them,' Mr. Budd warned.

'What about Detective Inspector Lane?' Telford asked. 'Might he have alerted them already?'

'They may have been alerted or they may not, which is a risk we have to take,' Mr. Budd replied. 'Lane was working undercover and would have been very careful not to give away his true identity. I don't know the circumstances that led to him bein' on the river; I wish I did. But one thing is certain — if they spot uniforms, we'll scare 'em off and we won't achieve anythin'. This has to be unofficial.'

'Incognito,' added Telford.

Mr. Budd scratched the back of his head thoughtfully. 'Yes, that's a very good word, Inspector — incognito. We need a couple in plain clothes posing as shop window dressers. They can enquire about mannequins for a London store — acting quite normal, but keepin' their eyes open for anything unusual.'

When Telford and Mr. Budd got back to the canteen, they explained the plan to Superintendent Ramsay.

'This is very much your ongoing investigation, Superintendent, though I'm sorry you've lost a key man,' Ramsay replied. 'We're obviously only a small part of this, but we're on the spot as it were, and I'd be pleased to assist in any way I can. Since the collision with the barge, Constables Bentley and Larkin are without a boat for at least a week while it undergoes repair. That damned barge tore the fendering off and severely damaged the decking, so they're free to work on this investigation.'

'That's very considerate of you, Ramsay,' said Mr. Budd. 'I think a man and a woman might be less likely to arouse suspicion.'

'Let me go, sir,' pleaded Glenda, overhearing. She'd immediately made up her mind this was exactly what she wanted to do.

Bentley looked horrified, and before he could stop himself intervened, forgetting his rank. 'You ought to be resting after the shock you've just — '

He broke off as Glenda sprang to her feet. 'I don't need to rest, Joe,' she objected firmly, her eyes blazing. 'I need to find out why my father died and do something about it — anything to take my mind off what's just happened. Rest is the last thing I feel like right now. Doing something worthwhile and positive is the best cure for grief.'

Her words were more poignant than any tears. Mr. Budd understood just what she meant. He nodded with sympathy and understanding, casting a meaningful glance at Ramsay and Telford. 'It can be a true fact, Miss Lane — work is the antidote to sorrow,' he agreed supportively.

Glenda looked at Ramsay and Telford with a steely determination they had not seen before. 'My father died in the line of duty,' she said, humbling all those present. 'I'll feel a lot better continuing that line of duty and assisting with this investigation. Please give me something to do.'

'Would you agree to Constables Bentley and Lane going along to this Studios place in plain clothes?' suggested Mr. Budd, seeing that both Ramsay and Telford were doubtful. 'They could pose as shop window dressers for a London store.'

'Are you certain you're up to it, Lane?' Ramsay asked her, not at all convinced.

'Yes I am. Obviously it's been a terrible shock. The one important thing I can do in my father's memory is to assist in whatever way I can to bring the people responsible for his death to justice. I assure you, I'll be perfectly fine.' She stuck her chin forward. 'You can rely on that.'

Ramsay smiled at her pluck and looked at Telford for assurance before he would commit to her being involved.

Glenda was already thinking about the assignment. 'I'll need to change into casual clothes.'

'That's quite right, Lane,' agreed Telford, suspicious of her quick recovery but going along with her resolve. 'You'll need to go home and prepare.' He looked at his watch. 'Bentley, you get some rest; you've been on duty all night. Both of you meet me back here at four o'clock in plain clothes.'

It was proposed that Glenda would adopt the name Miss Joan Fielding and make an appointment for four-thirty that afternoon to visit Natural Art Studios in Mews Street. She would be posing as a shop window dresser for 'Jessops', a well-known Knightsbridge store. Joe Bentley would accompany her as Mr. Jack Davenport, her assistant. Thames Division contacted the owners of Jessops, who, as a temporary cover, agreed to add the two assumed names to their staff list. A dedicated telephone line was allocated that would be answered by a member of Thames Division pretending to represent the store as a precaution in the event someone at Natural Art Studios sought to verify their visitors' credentials.

Within fifteen minutes of the appointment being made, there was a return call to confirm it. Miss Joan Fielding and Mr. Jack Davenport had been checked out and found to be genuine.

⋆   ⋆   ⋆

The police surgeon Dr. Melthorne, arrived; a dapper little man wearing a bowler hat and carrying a silver-topped cane. He briefly examined the body of the deceased detective.

'Those pulled from the river aren't normally as fresh as this one,' he commented in the superintendent's ear as Bradshaw began taking photographs of the body from all angles. 'Where was the body found?'

Mr. Budd quietly explained who the corpse was and how Derek Lane had been found floating at Butler's Wharf Pier, downstream of Tower Bridge. He went over the circumstances that he believed had led to the detective's death, including the collision with the runaway barge.

Melthorne continued his examination in a more respectful manner, explaining that the massive blunt force trauma on the left side of the forehead might have been the cause of death, in which case the time of the collision with the barge would determine the time of death.

'That would be five-thirty this mornin',' Mr. Budd informed him.

'The detective inspector might have been knocked unconscious by the impact of the barge, alive when thrown into the river, only to have subsequently drowned,' Melthorne pointed out. 'The water, being very cold this time of the year, paralyses the nervous system, making a recovery almost impossible.'

'Could he 'ave been killed before the collision?'

Dr. Melthorne pursed his lips. 'It's possible. The time of death is difficult to pin down. As I say, the river would have chilled the body quickly. Are you suggesting he was murdered, Superintendent?'

'I'm not suggesting anythin',' Mr. Budd retorted evasively.

Melthorne closed up his medical case

in a gesture of finality. 'The body can go to the morgue for the autopsy. We'll know a lot more after that.'

Telford glanced at Mr. Budd to check if he had any further questions.

'There's not much else we can do for him now,' the superintendent remarked sadly, thanking the medical examiner.

Telford guided Mr. Budd over to a pile of wreckage that was all that remained of the boat they believed Derek Lane had been rowing. He pointed to a faded number on the prow. 'Unless I'm very much mistaken, this boat belongs to a Mr. George Stacey. He's got a small yard at Bermondsey Wall.'

'Then it'd be a good idea to pay Mr. Stacey a visit,' Mr. Budd suggested.

Telford nodded in agreement. 'Exactly what I was thinking, Superintendent. I've a launch standing by.'

Mr. Budd remained silent as he looked suspiciously at the ramp that led at a steep angle to the moored police boats. He didn't trust the fast-flowing steely waters of the river, knowing how treacherous they could be. Nevertheless, despite his reservations, it was a quick and uneventful ride in a supervision launch from Wapping across to Bermondsey Wall on the opposite bank of the river. It was nearly ten o'clock by the time Mr. Budd arrived with Telford at George Stacey's boat yard, and the supervision launch moored up at a floating pontoon. The walkway that led up to the yard was little more than a couple of planks with rope guides.

Telford sought the attention of two men who were hauling a boat up the slipway. 'Where can we find George Stacey?' he demanded with authority.

'In his office,' answered one of the men, immediately suspicious of Telford's uniform. He jerked his thumb at the two story boathouse. 'I'll show yer.'

Telford and Mr. Budd followed the man up a short flight of stairs to a small landing and then into a large room with a window overlooking the river. It was a chaotic room of charts, stacks of unfiled papers, and boxes of various marine paraphernalia. The inner wall was dominated by a large map of the River Thames from Tower Bridge to Woolwich. Slumped behind a desk, on which sat several empty mugs and a half-empty bottle of Johnny Walker, was an untidy middle-aged man with slicked-back hair. The office smelled like a distillery. Telford made the introduction.

'Mr. Stacey, this is Superintendent Budd of Scotland Yard.'

Stacey forced a thin smile and grunted. He was obviously not pleased about being disturbed. 'Scotland Yard,' he mumbled. 'For what do I owe this honour?'

'In the early hours of this mornin',' began Mr. Budd, 'one of your boats was involved in a collision with a Thames lighter, a drifter.'

'A drifter — where did this happen?' Stacey demanded.

'Near Tower Bridge,' Telford answered.

George Stacey raised his eyebrows and leaned forward irritably, resting his elbows on the ring-marked desktop. 'Do you have a number for the boat?'

'Thirty-seven,' answered Telford.

Stacey grabbed a worn ledger and dragged it towards him. Tearing through some well-thumbed pages, he consulted the latest entries. 'Thirty-seven was hired out to a Mr. Frank Jepson two days ago.'

'Did yer know this man you hired the boat to?' asked Mr. Budd.

'No,' said Stacey, shaking his head.

Mr. Budd's brows drew together. 'You rented a boat to someone you've never seen before?'

Stacey looked affronted. 'Well, he left a handsome deposit.'

'I'm afraid your boat's damaged beyond repair, Mr. Stacey,' Telford informed him. 'I hope you have insurance.'

George Stacey's face twisted up into something quite unrecognisable.

'What did he look like, this Frank Jepson?' Mr. Budd asked.

Stacey raised his eyebrows. 'I dunno.'

'Try harder,' Mr. Budd suggested sternly.

'Well, let me think for a minute.' Stacey reached for the whisky bottle and then thought better of it. 'I don't remember him very well. He was weedy-lookin' with a thin face and wore a cap, but I think he had red hair on account of his sideburns. I don't see many men with red hair.'

★   ★   ★

At the Surrey docks, Mr. Budd and Telford met up with the two customs men who had carried out the recent inspection of cargo on board the *Gelderland* prior to unloading. First sight of the 1500-ton ship caused Mr. Budd to realise the mannequins were small beer compared to the rest of the cargo and probably of little significance to Captain Issak Slaatama. They climbed up the gangway and were shown into the captain's cabin.

They didn't have long to wait until Slaatama entered. Their immediate impression was of something round and greasy. His shirt was blotched with sweat stains and his trousers were held up by faded red braces. His black hair was swept back from his forehead and gathered at the back of his neck in a ponytail. His face, dominated by a huge nose reddened by alcohol, was mean and suspicious, on account of two small dark eyes, like raisins, that were constantly on the move, darting back and forth from Mr. Budd to Telford. They finally locked onto the two customs men, and a glimmer of recognition crossed his features.

'Vell, gentlemen, vat can I do for you?' he asked in a squeaky voice.

'We'd like to look at your cargo manifest for this last voyage,' Telford requested stiffly. 'In particular, the shop window mannequins.'

Captain Slaatama swaggered to a shelf and, with an arm like a hock of ham, took down a thick file. He banged the file on his desk and began flicking through several pages, uttering grunting noises until he reached the page he was searching for, when he slapped a fat hand down on it.

'Here it is — twenty mannequins from Vandekkan packed in vooden crates, imported by Natural Art Studios, Mews Street, London.' He looked at the two customs men accusingly. 'You examined them, and here is your clearance stamp.'

He lifted out a page detailing the mannequin shipment between two sausage-like fingers and waved it in the air.

'May I look at that sheet, please?' Mr. Budd requested.

The captain of the *Gelderland* swung round on Mr. Budd pugnaciously. 'And who are you?' he demanded.

'Superintendent Budd of Scotland Yard,' answered the big man solemnly, his eyes narrowing.

Slaatama grimaced as he handed over the sheet. 'Alvays trouble,' he grumbled. 'Alvays trouble to take up my time. Is there something wrong?'

Mr. Budd glanced down the list of twenty dummies classed as the Veritas range. V for Veritas, he assumed. He noticed there was an initial in the column by two of the other dummies, but no initial by the one listed as V7. He turned to one of the customs men and handed him the sheet. 'These are your initials?' he asked.

'Yes, sir, we always do a random check,' explained the customs man, returning the sheet. 'We looked inside the two that I initialled.'

'And you found nothing inside 'em?'

'That's right, sir. We'd have impounded them if we had.'

'They found nothing because there was nothing. I run a clean ship,' boasted Captain Slaatama arrogantly, now he was in the clear. 'Every two veeks ve bring in a consignment from Vandekkan. Every time, a random check is made and nothing has ever been found.' He shrugged his big rounded shoulders. 'There is nothing to find.'

Mr. Budd looked at the two men from customs for corroboration.

'That's quite correct, sir,' they both replied.

There was nothing further to be achieved, and Mr. Budd might have thought his visit was a waste of time if it wasn't for his intuition that something was wrong. He wondered if it was possible the customs men were in on it — however, on further investigation, they explained the same custom men seldom carried out a customs check twice running. They operated on a rota system, a deliberate procedure designed to prevent any familiarity with a ship's crew that might lead to the acceptance of bribes or shady deals.

As the supervision boat took Mr. Budd up river to Charing Cross Pier, from where he planned to walk back to his office at Scotland Yard, he scanned the choppy waters of the Thames uneasily. The wind was fresh, bringing the aromas of the river to his nostrils and catching the tip of his cigar, fanning it to a red glow. He idly watched the cars and buses crossing Tower Bridge like toys. He blew out a stream of smoke and watched it dispersed by the wind, as he tried to work out how counterfeit notes could be smuggled into the country in dummies that were checked at random by customs officers. Something was wrong here — something was very wrong. He was annoyed that he had no idea what it was.

'Don't worry about formalities, Telford,' he said to the detective inspector as he clambered off the boat at Charing Cross Pier. 'If yer turn up anything, please call me directly. I'm going to make a telephone call to Interpol and attack this criminal gang at the source. I want to know where they get the paper and where they print the notes — I'm goin' to follow up the Dutch connection.'

⋆   ⋆   ⋆

Later that afternoon, Glenda Lane and Joe Bentley stood at the entrance to St. Katherine's Docks. Wrapped up against the cold in coats and scarves, they gazed out upon the icy waters flowing upriver at five miles per hour and listened to the waves lapping relentlessly at the outer walls of the dock. They inhaled the oily wet-dog smell of the river. In less than an hour, it would be high tide and the dock gates would open.

'This is where it happened, somewhere near here,' Glenda said sadly. 'I keep asking myself what my dad was doing on the river in the fog at that hour of the morning with that mannequin.' She clenched her gloved fists. 'What possible purpose could he have had? I need closure — I need to *know*, Joe.'

Joe Bentley hung his head. He felt responsible somehow, though of course he wasn't. 'If we'd got there earlier, we'd have overtaken the barge, and might have spotted your father in the boat and prevented that terrible accident from happening.'

Shaking her head, Glenda took his arm and looked up at him with a worried frown. 'Don't blame yourself, Joe. He'd tested his luck a few times and it finally ran out. I doubt if there was anything anyone could have done.'

She turned around and looked up Mews Street, taking in the ruins of those warehouses badly damaged by bombing during the war. Once thriving, now they were abandoned, sandwiched between the street and the dockside, awaiting demolition. The light was fading, and a low mist was creeping over the river, thickening into patches of dense fog. They could hear the fog horns booming from the Pool of London. It was very cold and grey.

Glenda shivered.

'I don't feel comfortable with you going to this studio place,' Bentley said protectively. 'We're unarmed, and it could be dangerous if we run into someone who . . .'

Glenda squeezed his arm. Bentley felt his pulse quicken at this small intimacy.

'That's the whole point, Joe. I *want* to meet them. Stop worrying — they don't know who we really are, and we have a legitimate appointment. It's not as if we were breaking and entering.'

They had another five minutes until their appointment, and slowly began to saunter up the street.

'It feels strange walking with you out of uniform, Joe,' she said, glancing up at him with an admiring smile. 'Like we're on a date.'

Bentley smiled at her in return. 'We *are* on a date, Glenda — to check out some spooky mannequins.'

'They *are* a bit spooky, aren't they? That one in the evidence room staring at me with those bright blue eyes, like she's reading my mind.' She gave a little shiver. 'I wanted to cover her up.'

As they approached Natural Art Studios, they saw a track leading down the side of the building and a lower storage area projecting out the back. They paused and looked down the track, which opened out onto a loading area between the back of the building and the edge of the dock.

'That's a back way onto the dock for loading and unloading,' Bentley said. 'I'm tempted to take a quick look.'

'If we're caught snooping, it'll blow our cover,' Glenda warned. 'We can always come back later.'

The front of the building was a two-storey red brick tower. Wide steps went up to an archway that framed imposing double oak doors.

'Let's get this over with, Miss Fielding,' Bentley said, starting up the steps with Glenda following.

'Shall I ring the bell, Mr. Davenport?' she asked, glancing at him for approval.

'I think that would be advisable, Miss Fielding,' he answered with a grin that barely disguised his nervousness.

She pushed a large domed ceramic button with the word 'press' on it in black letters and gave Joe a fatalistic look. From somewhere inside came a persistent ringing. 'No going back now,' she whispered.

They could hear heavy bolts being withdrawn and then a key turning in the lock. The oak doors swung open a few inches. In the narrow gap stood a big muscular man with unruly hair the colour of dirty straw. An ugly scar ran up the left side of his face to the corner of his eye. He spoke with a Dutch accent.

'Can I help you?'

'I'm Miss Fielding, and this is my assistant Mr. Davenport,' answered Glenda confidently. 'I made an appointment to look at mannequins. I'm from Jessops.'

The man with the scarred face looked them up and down suspiciously and narrowed his eyes, making them feel uncomfortable, like the imposters they were. 'This is the right place then,' he grunted.

He swung the heavy doors fully open and stood aside to let them enter. As soon as they were inside, he shoved the doors shut with a bang that reverberated throughout the building. Feeling like prisoners, they waited in the high ceilinged vestibule while he bolted and relocked the doors and then disappeared up circular stone steps that curved out of sight to another level. Daylight filtered in through narrow barred windows. At the far end of the vestibule, a wide archway to their right opened onto a long vaulted warehouse with brick walls lined with shop mannequins of all shapes and sizes, like a nude army waiting for action. Double doors stood open at the far end, leading into another warehouse with yet more mannequins. They could hear voices coming from the floor above.

'This is weird,' whispered Glenda. 'That man gives me the creeps.' As they wandered into the vaulted display area, she said, looking around in disappointment, 'These are very ordinary.'

'They look like standard shop dummies to me,' Bentley agreed. 'I don't see any like our woman, V7.'

'How disappointing for you!' she joked.

The sound of footsteps descending the

steps from above caused them to swing round. A man was walking towards them. He was scrawny, almost emaciated, with a hard rodent face and red sideburns, topped with a mop of red hair. He was wearing a pinstriped suit that was obviously too big for him. He didn't look at all happy to see them and appeared irritated at the interruption. There was no personal interaction, no warm greeting with a smile, none of the techniques of a professional salesman.

'You must be Mr. Silk?' Glenda asked in her sweetest voice.

The man nodded, forcing a thin smile that almost immediately disappeared. 'I am, yes. You're from Jessops?'

'Yes, we are,' she confirmed, ignoring the awkwardness of the situation.

'And you're lookin' for — '

Glenda swallowed and hoped she would sound convincing. 'We're designing a new window display for our summer collection and we're after the new realistic look — something that will stand out and attract attention, stopping people as they walk past.'

Mr. Silk strode over to a group of mannequins. 'These are from our latest range,' he said.

Glenda and Joe pretended to take an interest. The mannequins had painted faces and wigs but looked cheap. None possessed the sculpted realism and make-up of the seventh virgin.

'How many were you looking for?' Silk asked.

'Twelve,' said Glenda. 'A round dozen.'

Mr. Silk raised his eyebrows. 'Sale or hire?'

'Oh, we'd want to buy them,' replied Glenda positively. She wrinkled her nose at the dummies on offer. 'This type isn't quite what we're looking for, Mr. Silk,' she told him, exaggerating her disappointment. 'We've noticed some of our competitors are using mannequins that are so realistic they really demand the attention of passers-by who stop and stare. Those are the type we want.'

'These are all we have,' Mr. Silk informed her without apology.

Glenda looked crestfallen. 'How disappointing — we were told your company supplied the more realistic models and that's why we made the appointment.'

Mr. Silk shrugged his shoulders. 'I'm sorry you've had a wasted journey.'

Bentley, on the pretext of looking at a row of featureless mannequins, had been sidling over towards the other display warehouse while Glenda and Mr. Silk were talking. At the far end was a loading bay that obviously opened onto the area out the back by the dockside. Beside the main doors was a smaller door. Light came from two long skylights that ran its length. He entered before Mr. Silk could stop him, his attention immediately arrested by stacks of wooden crates piled up against one wall. Some of the crates had been opened, and he saw a crowbar lying next to a pile of splintered wood. Beyond the crates was a surreal pile of platinum-blonde V7 heads; there must have been about twenty of them. They were without their bodies, like victims of the guillotine, their sightless eyes staring in all directions. Despite being made of plaster, they possessed the same creepy life-like quality as the one he'd pulled out of the Thames that morning.

Bentley performed a quick calculation — if each of the dummies contained the same number of packages as the seventh virgin, someone must have retrieved about two hundred thousand pounds from the missing bodies. That represented a considerable amount of money by anyone's reckoning, and he wondered if it was it still in the building or if it had been moved. He went over to the pile of heads, making a big show of discovering them.

'Look, Miss Fielding!' he exclaimed enthusiastically, pointing at the heads. 'Do come over here — I think these are exactly what we're looking for!'

Glenda ignored Mr. Silk and hurried over to Bentley. 'Oh, yes!' She exclaimed, looking at the pile of heads. 'Those are the very ones!' She turned accusingly to Mr. Silk. 'You do have some after all!'

Mr. Silk came up to them with a frown.

'But they don't have any bodies,' she remarked with wide-eyed innocence.

'Bit awkward with no bodies,' agreed Bentley, hoping he sounded as foolish as he was trying to be.

'Those are rejects,' Mr. Silk told them forcefully, his lip curled back. 'They're damaged goods and not for sale.'

Glenda looked crestfallen. 'What do you call this type?' she asked, peering closely at one of the heads.

'Veritas,' Mr. Silk replied, breathing heavily. 'But we've sold out.'

'Will you be getting more of them?' she enquired.

'Not for another two weeks,' he answered gruffly.

'Oh!' Glenda feigned disappointment. 'Well, never mind, we can wait two weeks. Tell me, Mr. Silk, are they all platinum-blondes, or is there variation in hair colour?'

'We have brunettes and redheads, short- or long-haired,' Silk answered.

'What about men?' Glenda asked. 'It's nice to have couples.'

'The full Veritas range includes men, women and children, but not for two weeks,' he reiterated irritably. 'I'm sorry if you've had a wasted journey.'

Bentley quickly worked out that if they

had a consignment of mannequins stuffed with banknotes every two weeks, about two hundred thousand pounds at a time, it wouldn't take long for millions of pounds of fake banknotes to get into circulation.

Mr. Silk began escorting them back to the main entrance.

'I don't think it's been a wasted visit at all,' said Glenda. 'Now we know where to come. Tell me, who was that man who opened the doors to us?'

'The Dutchman.' Mr. Silk answered, then broke off abruptly, giving her a suspicious stare.

'If you're not available, do we get in touch with *him*?' Glenda asked sweetly.

'Certainly not! He doesn't work here. He's only . . . ' His voice trailed off as he tried to hide his agitation by pulling back the bolts and unlocking the doors. A blast of cold air swept in. They walked past him and Glenda paused on the top step, turning back.

'Thank you for your time, Mr. Silk,' she said. 'We both look forward to seeing you again in two weeks.'

'I'll notify you,' answered Silk, slamming shut the big doors.

In the short time they had been inside the building, the light had faded, and it was now dusk. They felt the bitter chill on their faces. As they started down the steps, Glenda took Bentley's arm.

'That was weird,' she commented, giggling. 'Mr. Silk has to be the worst salesman I've ever met.'

'The whole setup was a sham,' Bentley said. 'The company must have changed hands. I can't imagine they've operated like that for long. You're quite right — Silk and that Dutchman chap have no idea how to deal with customers, and I doubt any of the big London stores have been back there recently.'

'That's very obvious,' Glenda agreed.

They walked up Mews Street in the opposite direction to the way they had come, heading towards Tower Hill.

'Careless leaving those heads for us to see, don't you think?'

Bentley shrugged. 'Crooks make mistakes or they wouldn't get caught.'

'I wonder how long they've been

94

bringing those mannequins into the country, Joe.'

'I've worked out how much they're raking in every two weeks.' He told her his calculations.

'I can't imagine that amount of money.'

'I think they bought that company to have a bona fide address to take the mannequins to after unloading them at the docks. They wanted somewhere that wouldn't look suspicious if there was any sort of investigation.'

'But there *was* an investigation. My father was investigating, and look what happened to him!'

Bentley said nothing, not wishing her to dwell on the accident.

'I'll check if the ownership has changed recently when we get back,' she offered. 'We've found out one thing — V doesn't mean virgin; it stands for Veritas.'

'The 'truth' range,' said Bentley.

'Silk didn't like it when you spotted those other mannequin heads. Did you see the look on his face? He could barely conceal his anger.'

'They knew we were coming,' said

Bentley. 'If they hadn't wanted us to see them, why didn't they hide them?'

'That's what I keep asking myself.'

They were stopped by two muffled bangs sounding from where they had come.

'Did you hear that?' said Bentley, swinging round on his heel and listening intently.

'Those sounded like gunshots!' Glenda exclaimed.

★   ★   ★

The Dutchman warmed his hands on a paraffin stove in the warehouse office while he finalised in his mind what he would do. He was convinced the two visitors were coppers — he could tell them a mile away. He dialled a number and reported the visit to the person on the other end of the line and then listened carefully to his instructions. They had attracted the attention of the police, and it was time to cover all tracks and disappear.

He put on a Gabardine coat and

grabbing the keys of his launch off the desktop, slipped them into a pocket. He unlocked a desk drawer and took out an automatic, keeping it concealed as he heard Silk ascending the stairs.

'Those were busies or else my name isn't Percival Silk,' he announced as he entered the office. 'When I agreed to this, Van der Horst, it didn't include getting this close to the perlice. That was not part of our deal.'

The Dutchman nodded as he slipped off the safety catch. 'This place has outlived its usefulness,' he replied coldly, levelling the automatic at Silk's chest. 'So have you, my friend.' He cold-bloodedly shot him twice through the heart.

Immediately, he picked up the paraffin stove and carried it out of the office to the head of the steps and went to a small storage area to fetch a drum of paraffin, which he carried back to the office. Tipping the drum on its side, he opened the tap and allowed half the fuel to spew over the floor and the dead body of Silk. Taking the drum with him, he swung the lit stove into the office and watched it burst into flames as it crashed to the floor. Then he hurried down the steps and through to the warehouse, where he poured the rest of the paraffin over the broken crates and the mannequin heads. He struck a match and watched them burn.

⋆   ⋆   ⋆

Joe Bentley stared back along Mews Street but couldn't see any movement.

'Be careful, Joe,' Glenda warned.

This was a defining moment in Bentley's life, when he realised he cared for Glenda and knew she cared for him. But he had no time to dwell on this realisation because he needed to concentrate on the job at hand.

'It's best you go on home now, Glenda,' he suggested protectively. 'I'll stay here and keep an eye on that place. I'm sure that's where the shots came from. If anyone leaves, I'll follow them and see where it leads.'

Glenda's eyes glittered with a steely determination as she looked up at him.

'I'm staying with you Joe,' she insisted.

Joe objected immediately. 'That's a crazy idea.'

Glenda was adamant. 'One of those men has a gun and you don't.'

'It's too dangerous.'

'You won't change my mind, Joe.'

She spoke firmly, Bentley knew no amount of arguing would change her mind. They cut through to the quayside, stole along the back of the Mews Street buildings, and eventually came to a bombed-out warehouse where from the ruins they could overlook the back of Natural Art Studios. They crouched behind a collapsed wall and, making themselves as comfortable as they could in the circumstances, waited for any sign of movement.

They didn't have to wait long. The Dutchman, his coat tails flapping, darted out of the rear door and ran towards the quayside, where he disappeared from view.

Making sure Glenda was properly concealed in case the Dutchman returned, Bentley hurried after him, bent double to keep a low profile. He reached the quay in time to see the Dutchman unhitch a mooring rope and board a sleek black launch with a black rose outlined in red painted on the prow. Taking his keys from his coat pocket, the Dutchman inserted a key in the ignition, starting the twin engines. He allowed himself a thin smile of gratification as he heard them growl into life. He switched on the navigation lights and cast off, opening the throttle and accelerating rapidly out of the docks on the high tide. Heading out into the river, the launch disappeared into the fog.

Bentley ran back to Glenda. 'Did you see that?' he asked her in frustration. 'He got away on a boat.'

'If only *we* had a boat,' she said, sharing his annoyance.

'That launch of his is a proper little beauty,' he told her, unable to disguise his enthusiasm. 'I reckon it could outrun anything on the river. None of our boats could catch him.'

Glenda pointed at the rear doors of the warehouse. Smoke was escaping from them, and in an upstairs window was a flickering glow.

'Look Joe, there's a fire!' she said in alarm.

Bentley was already running towards the door through which they'd seen the Dutchman leave. 'He's set fire to the place!' he shouted back.

Glenda ran after him. 'Those *were* shots we heard — Mr. Silk might still be inside!'

The glow in the upstairs window suddenly blossomed into leaping white and orange flames. 'If he is, there's not much we can do for him,' Bentley remarked grimly.

Glenda looked dismayed. 'We have to try to do something.'

Bentley tried the small door. The Dutchman in his hurry had left it unlocked, and it opened easily. He'd only opened it an inch when a blast of heat burst out, forcing him to kick it shut and beat a hasty retreat. There was a raging inferno inside.

'We can't go in there!' Bentley shouted, shielding his eyes. He stared at her helplessly. 'It would be certain suicide. There's no hope for Mr. Silk if he's still inside.'

'This is terrible,' she said. 'There must be something we can do. Where's the fire brigade?'

'They'll be on their way. You can see this fire from across the river and someone will have called them. This has been deliberately torched using an accelerant.'

The rear loading doors of the warehouse were turning black, the wood splintering and crackling with the heat. As they watched helplessly, the loading doors burst into flames. Billows of smoke began to wreathe the building. Showers of sparks shot skywards as parts of the roof collapsed. The jangling bells of fire engines reached their ears and two fire engines came down the side of the building, pulling up by the dockside. By the time the firemen had prepared their equipment and got organised, the warehouse was well and truly ablaze and beyond saving. As the water from their hoses struck the burning building, great billows of steam hissed up into the cold air.

After what seemed an age, the searchlight of a Thames Division duty boat broke through the fog, heading towards the entrance to the docks. Outlined against the conflagration, Glenda and Bentley waved to the crew, who flashed the searchlight on and off in recognition. Mike Larkin waved to them from the stern of the duty boat as he prepared to tie up, taking the Dutchman's recently vacated mooring. Sergeant Arnold Reeves clambered up onto the dock, followed by Constable Potts. Mike Larkin stayed aboard.

'Are you two all right?' Reeves asked. 'Tell me what happened.'

Bentley rapidly explained the events that had taken place since their arrival that afternoon up until the Dutchman escaped in his high speed launch.

'We think there's a dead man still in there,' added Glenda. 'The Dutchman shot him.'

Sergeant Reeves looked at both of them with caution. 'Do you know that for a fact? What evidence 'ave you got that this Dutchman killed someone? Did you witness 'im pulling the trigger?'

'We heard the shots,' replied Glenda defensively.

'I'm pretty certain he shot this man Silk before torching the place,' corroborated Bentley.

'But you didn't see 'im do it?' persisted Reeves. 'That won't hold up in a court of law.'

'Neither of us was a witness inside the building,' Glenda agreed reluctantly with exasperation. 'We were down the street when we heard the shots. We rushed back here and saw the Dutchman run out the back door over there.' She pointed to where smoke was escaping through a burned-out hole in the wall of the warehouse. 'He escaped in his launch as the building went up in flames. Any evidence inside has been conveniently destroyed. Pretty conclusive, wouldn't you say, Sergeant?'

'Got any idea where this Dutch feller's gone?' asked Reeves.

'None at all,' Bentley answered. 'He

was headed downriver.'

Sergeant Reeves wrestled with himself to come to a decision.

'He's getting as far away from here as quickly as possible, I should imagine, while we stand here arguing,' Glenda warned impatiently.

'Bentley, get on the radio and report what's 'appened to Telford,' Reeves ordered, starting off towards the fire engines. 'I'll 'ave a word with the fire officer.'

Mike Larkin stood on the deck, grinning up at them.

'Sergeant Reeves can be a bit slow at times,' he admitted with a wink. 'He likes to do things by the book.'

Glenda and Bentley climbed down onto the deck of the duty boat, and Bentley gave a concise report of the afternoon's events to Detective Inspector Telford over the radio. Telford agreed to put out an all-stations alert for the Dutchman.

5

On his way to Scotland Yard from Charing Cross Pier, Mr. Budd stopped off at a pub for a quick lunch consisting of a cheese and pickle sandwich washed down with a pint of beer. Arriving at the Yard, he nodded to the constable on duty and ponderously climbed the stairs to his cheerless office. He hung up his hat and coat, produced one of his atrocious black cigars from his waistcoat pocket, and lowered his prodigious bulk into his chair.

He peeled the band carefully off the cigar, turning it slowly between two fingers, while he considered what his next move should be. Searching around for a box of matches, he found one, and striking a match, lighted the cigar. He exhaled a cloud of smoke and watched it fan out over the ceiling. When the office was satisfyingly full of the foul-smelling smoke, he drifted into sleepy contemplation before busily making copious notes

106

for half an hour. He checked through the notes carefully to make certain he had left nothing out and then instructed the switchboard to put through a call to the International Criminal Police Organisation, more commonly known as Interpol. He spoke to an opposite number at their headquarters in France for nearly twenty minutes.

Just as he was considering going home, new information came in from Detective Inspector Telford updating him on the latest results of their operations. He read through Constable Bentley's description of the Dutchman and Mr. Silk, pausing when he got to 'rat-faced' and 'red hair'. It looked like Mr. Silk was the man who'd rented the boat that Derek Lane had been rowing across the river.

As he continued reading through Bentley's report, he realised it was unlikely that he would get to interview Mr. Silk. He agreed with Joe Bentley and Glenda Lane that it looked as if the Dutchman was covering his tracks and had set fire to the building to destroy any evidence, including the body of Silk. The sighting of the mannequin heads suggested Derek Lane had discovered an important part of the counterfeiters' operation. Mr. Budd didn't expect to see any more mannequins stuffed with packets of fivers. He was certain the gang would find a new way to smuggle the counterfeit notes into the country.

Sergeant Leek entered his office wearing a thin smile on his usually melancholy features. Budd seldom saw Leek smile, but on the rare occasions he did, he found it rather disquieting. Leek produced his notebook with an unnatural flourish.

'Natural Art Studios was taken over from the previous owners eight months ago,' he began, bursting with exuberance.

'I expected as much,' interrupted Mr. Budd, impatiently scratching his chin. 'Who took 'em over?'

'I was just comin' to that,' protested Leek in a hurt voice. His joyful moment faded away to be replaced by his usual long face. 'The current owner is a Peter Van der Horst of 23 Paradise Street. It's in Bermondsey.'

'Now we're getting' somewhere,' said Mr. Budd, blowing out a cloud of rank smoke and allowing himself a glimmer of satisfaction. 'That's very interestin' — very interestin' indeed.'

There was little to show in Mr. Budd's expression the elation with which this news filled him. Events were rapidly providing facts; and he knew it was facts, and only facts, which would secure him convictions.

The mannequins came into the Port of London from Amsterdam aboard a Dutch ship the *Gelderland* — fact. They were then transported to a warehouse in Mews Street, near St. Katherine's Docks, where Glenda Lane and Joe Bentley met a man they called the Dutchman and a Mr. Silk — fact. The Dutchman torched the warehouse and disappeared — fact. Both the Dutchman and Silk were part of the organisation smuggling the counterfeit money — nearly a fact. Silk hired a boat from George Stacey — nearly a fact. How did Derek Lane come to be rowing that same boat across the river at five thirty in the morning? — a mystery that needed to be solved. Peter Van der Horst was a Dutch name, and Mr. Budd had every reason to assume Peter Van der Horst and the Dutchman were one and the same person.

'Order an unmarked car to take us to that address in Bermondsey without delay,' he said to Sergeant Leek, heaving his bulk out of his chair with surprising agility. 'Better get an armed police sergeant to come with us,' he added. He put on his coat and taking a torch out of a desk drawer slipped it into a pocket. 'Let's see what we can find out about Mr. Peter Van der Horst.'

Grabbing his hat, he placed it firmly on his head as he went out the door. He briefed the armed police sergeant, Peters, and the driver of the black Wolseley. He sat on the back seat next to Sergeant Leek, and taking out another of his evil-smelling black cigars, sniffed at it. If he was correct and the Dutchman and Peter Van der Horst were one and the same person, then the house they were speeding to was his home. But where exactly did Van der Horst fit in the chain of command? Who did he answer to? What happened to the fake bank notes when they were removed from the mannequins?

Another significant stage in the counterfeiters' operation was to launder the fake banknotes into circulation exchanging them for the real thing. Who organised that? His investigation was still long on conjecture and short on facts, but past experience had taught him that conjecture often paved the way to facts and a satisfactory conclusion.

The roads were busy, and over half an hour had passed before the car pulled up outside a small house at one end of Paradise Street.

★　★　★

When the Dutchman reached midstream, he steered the *Black Rose* downriver towards a Victorian Pub called The Angel. It was perched right on the waterfront in Rotherhithe Street, at the far end of Bermondsey Wall East. It was popular with watermen who often tied up their boats at the moorings and then climbed the steep steps up to the street level entrance.

As the familiar lights of the pub became visible between patches of fog, the Dutchman throttled the powerful engines back to a low burbling sound, then went into reverse, steering the launch expertly behind two barges so that it couldn't be seen from the river. He tied off and leapt up the steps to the street above. He ignored the inviting lights of the pub and hurried down Cathay Street to Paradise. Despite being in a hurry, the Dutchman was cautious as he approached his house, gripping the automatic in his coat pocket in case of trouble.

He let himself in by the back door, careful to avoid turning on any lights. He picked up a torch from a shelf in the scullery and by its light went down the hall turning right into his front room. Crossing to a dilapidated roll-top desk, he unlocked the top and rolled it back, exposing small drawers and pigeonholes stuffed with papers. He pulled out a centre drawer and, tipping its contents onto the desktop, began sifting through various items. He selected two passports and slipped them into his pocket. Then he flipped the drawer over and slid out a key that had been carefully concealed in a slot cut into the wood. He replaced the drawer, closed the roll top, and relocked it.

Dashing upstairs to his bedroom, he rummaged around in the base of a wardrobe and, pulling out an empty haversack, threw it over by the door. From a bedside drawer, he took a fully loaded clip for his automatic and put it in his pocket. He returned to the scullery with the haversack and let himself out the back door, shutting it behind him. He hurried down the garden to a dilapidated shed.

The door was half off its hinges and squeaked as he pushed it fully open and went inside. The door swung back to its former position with another squeak behind him. Avoiding piles of junk, he headed towards the back left corner and, clearing some hemp sacks out of the way, shone the beam of his torch on a square of rotting floorboards. He balanced the torch on a bucket while he lifted up a false floor to expose a steel safe hidden beneath. The safe was flat on its back and cemented into the ground.

He spun the combination lock and pulled the heavy safe door open. He worked quickly, taking out bundles of banknotes and stuffing them into the haversack. He had just finished his task when he heard a car draw up outside the house and the slamming of car doors.

His lips drew back in a snarl of anger and he hurriedly closed the safe, replacing the false floor and the hemp sacks. He pushed his haversack to the back of the shed as he heard heavy footsteps approaching the rear of the house. Turning off the torch, he took out his automatic and crouched in the dark, waiting . . .

★   ★   ★

Mr. Budd got out of the police car and stood surveying the property. The front windows had closed shutters through which there wasn't any sign of light.

'There doesn't appear ter be anyone at home,' he said.

He instructed his driver to wait in the car and sent Sergeant Peters around the back of the house with instructions to stop anyone who might try to leave. Accompanied by Leek, he walked up to the front door, where he paused, listening. Not hearing anything, he rapped sharply with the knocker.

As he expected, there was no answer.

'We'll take a look round the back,' he said to a weary and shivering Leek. He directed the powerful beam of his torch onto the side gate left open by Peters. Moving surprisingly quickly, he marched down the side of the house. Leek followed, struggling to catch up. The superintendent shone his torch over the back of the house, bringing its beam to rest upon a small scullery window.

'The place is empty,' remarked the melancholy sergeant.

Mr. Budd grunted with satisfaction as he swept his beam across a small overgrown garden. A dilapidated shed stood as a ghostly blur in the thin fog.

'Can you see anything down there?' Mr. Budd asked.

Sergeant Peters and Leek both turned away from the house to look in the direction in which the torch beam was pointing, and as they did so the big man heaved an elbow through the scullery window. Leek and Peters swung around in alarm at the sudden sound of breaking glass. Peters instinctively drew his firearm.

'I think there's been a break-in,' said Mr. Budd, shining his torch on the broken window. 'We'd better investigate!' He put his hand through the gap and opened the casement. 'In you go, Leek,' he instructed amiably.

'I can't get through there!' objected his sergeant.

Mr. Budd's big face broke into a smile. 'Of course yer can,' he said encouragingly. 'That's why yer were made so thin.'

Despite his protestations, the lean sergeant took off his coat and managed to worm his body through the window opening. Once inside, he located a light switch and the scullery was bathed with light. Leek opened the back door from the inside.

Mr. Budd instructed Sergeant Peters to remain outside on guard and to keep out of the light. 'It appears the Dutchman has an appetite for killing. He could be close by, and I 'ave no wish to provide him with any easy targets.'

Mr. Budd swiftly entered the house and handed Leek his coat.

The Dutchman watched these proceedings from his shed, alert for any opportunity to make his escape. He hadn't seen the sergeant draw his pistol, but as he passed across the light from the scullery window into darker shadow, he caught a glimpse of the gun in the policeman's hand. For the moment, he was trapped and had no alternative but to remain hidden in the shed or shoot his way out. He chose the former for the time being, but his nature was not totally averse to the latter.

More lights went on in the house as Mr. Budd and Sergeant Leek made a cursory search of the premises. The superintendent humphed with satisfaction as he found two jackets in an upstairs wardrobe tailored in Amsterdam. Finding nothing else of interest, he returned to the ground floor and gave his attention to the roll-top desk in the front room. He tried opening it, but the roll-top wouldn't budge.

'See if yer can find something to lever this open, will yer?' he asked Leek.

Leek hunted around in the kitchen, but the best thing he could find was a large knife; and the moment Mr. Budd applied any real pressure, the end snapped off.

'Maybe there's a crowbar or something like that down in that old shed,' suggested Mr. Budd, handing Leek his torch. ''Ave a look, will yer?'

Leek mumbled something incomprehensible and went outside. He gave a brief nod to Peters as he trudged down the garden.

The Dutchman watched the approaching light dancing towards him and retreated to the back of the shed. He perched on the haversack and pulled some sacking over himself, tensing up as footsteps stopped at the dilapidated shed door, which squeaked in protest as Leek pushed it further open and stepped over the threshold. The sergeant played the torch beam around the interior, illuminating some jerry cans, an old rusting mangle, a stack of garden tools, various bits of rope, and near the back by a cobwebbed window an axe balanced on a rusty nail. *The very tool*, Leek thought, heaving a sigh of relief that he had found something useful with which to bust open the roll-top desk.

He ventured deeper into the shed's interior, the old boards cracking and groaning as they bore his weight. As he reached out for the axe handle, his torch beam caught a couple of wooden fruit boxes, and beside them a shapeless pile of old sacking out of which protruded a foot. At first Leek thought it was an old discarded shoe, but as he directed his torch beam full onto it, he saw an ankle and part of a leg that disappeared beneath the sackcloth. His first thought was that he'd discovered a dead body.

As he moved closer to get a better look, the sacking sprang at him!

He opened his eyes in horror, dropped the torch and leapt backwards. The torch landed on the bare boards with a clatter and rolled away. Before he could gather his wits, a piece of sacking was pulled down over his head and drawn tight about his neck.

'Don't make a sound,' hissed the Dutchman through the sackcloth, close to Leek's ear.

'Wotcher want?' asked the astounded Leek, speaking with difficulty with the sackcloth stretched tightly over his face.

The Dutchman pressed the cold steel of his automatic into his captive's neck. 'I said not a sound!'

The Dutchman grabbed a length of rope with his free hand and double-looped it around Leek's throat, pulled the rope tight to hold the sacking firmly in place, and knotted it.

'Put your hands behind your back,' the Dutchman ordered in a low menacing voice. 'Do it now.'

Well aware of his helpless position,

Leek had no option but to do as he was told, and the Dutchman tied his wrists together.

'We're going to go for a walk,' hissed the Dutchman, picking up his haversack and slinging it over one shoulder. 'You do exactly as I tell you, or you get it first. How many are there?'

'Four,' mumbled Leek, finding it difficult to breathe because the rope was compressing his windpipe.

'One at the front?'

Leek grunted assent.

The Dutchman held Leek's neck in a vice-like grip, kicked open the shed door, and propelled him forward along the path.

★   ★   ★

Mr. Budd wondered what was keeping his sergeant. It didn't take long to look in a shed and see if there was anything useful. He went outside and accosted Peters.

'Have you seen my sergeant?' he asked.

Peters pointed to the bottom of the garden. 'He went down there.'

Mr. Budd had given Leek his torch, so he no longer had a portable light. 'I can't understand why it's taking him so long,' he grumbled. 'Have you got a torch?'

'Yes, sir,' answered the sergeant, taking one from a pocket.

Budd pointed to the shed. 'P'raps you'd shine it down there and see what's happened to 'im.'

As the constable directed the beam of his torch through thin fog onto the shed door, an extraordinary sight met their eyes. A hooded figure emerged and began stumbling towards them, with something bigger and darker close behind. Peters's mouth dropped open at the apparition.

'Blimey!' he exclaimed as he raised his pistol, unsure what to expect.

The Dutchman kept Leek between himself and the two policemen, thrusting the unfortunate sergeant forward as a human shield. It took Mr. Budd a couple of seconds to realise what was going on.

'If either of you tries anything, I'll shoot this man,' the Dutchman threatened. He appeared from behind Leek and waved his gun at an old blue chair by the back wall. 'Put any weapons, handcuffs and keys on that chair,' he instructed.

Mr. Budd had no doubt the Dutchman would carry out his threat. He reluctantly nodded assent to Peters, who placed his gun, handcuffs and a key on the chair as he'd been told.

Leek and the Dutchman came up to them. As the Dutchman put down his heavy haversack, the scar down the side of his face caught the light from the scullery window.

'What about you?' he asked Mr. Budd, threatening him with his automatic.

Mr. Budd shook his head.

The Dutchman stepped forward and picked up the things off the chair. He snapped one half of the bracelet around the superintendent's wrist. 'Handcuff your wrist to the copper with the other half,' he ordered.

'Yer only making this more difficult for yerself,' said Mr. Budd.

'Don't threaten me!' the Dutchman snarled. 'Do as I say!'

Mr. Budd reluctantly complied.

The Dutchman prodded Leek in the

ribs with his gun. 'Do you have cuffs?'

The sack-covered head nodded.

The Dutchman released his hold on Leek's neck and, taking the cuffs from the sergeant's pocket, put one half of the bracelet on Leek's wrist, leaving the other end dangling. He pushed Leek roughly up to the other two and swung him round so he could fasten the free end of the cuffs to Mr. Budd's other hand. When satisfied they were securely daisy-chained together, he lowered his gun and thrust his scarred face close to Mr. Budd.

'Who are you?' he demanded.

'Superintendent Robert Budd of Scotland Yard,' the big man answered, slowly and with all the authority he could muster. 'I expect you're Mr. Peter Van der Horst?'

'You got here quicker than I expected,' the Dutchman admitted. 'Now get inside!

The trio shuffled into the house.

'Go through to the front room,' ordered the Dutchman, shoving Sergeant Peters in the back.

The trio shuffled awkwardly along the hallway. Leek couldn't breathe properly or see where he was going, and kept bumping into the wall. The Dutchman bundled them into the front room and pushed them over to the roll-top desk.

'I'll tell you this, Mr. Scotland Yard,' the Dutchman sneered as he backed out of the room, 'you'll regret the day you messed with me. I don't like burglars, as you're about to find out.'

He left the room and, slamming the door shut, locked them in.

The moment they heard the key turn in the lock, they got busy. Leek fell to his knees so that Peters could get to work on the rope that secured the sacking around his head. The knots were tight, but gradually Peters's strong fingers unravelled them and tore off the sacking. Leek was red in the face with marks of the cloth deeply indented into the skin of his cheeks. He gulped in air gratefully, staring at the others in bewilderment.

'We've got to get out of here,' Mr. Budd warned urgently, pulling them towards the shuttered window. The shutters were bolted at the top which, given their present predicament, made them impossible to reach.

The Dutchman went straight to the kitchen and took down a couple of paraffin lamps from a shelf. Striking a match, he lit them and carried them out into the hallway. He threw one of them at a hall table and hat stand that stood between the front door and the front room. The glass broke and the paraffin spilled out and ignited, sending flames licking up the hat stand, the legs of the table, and creating a lake of fire as it flowed under the door where the three policemen were imprisoned. He threw the second lamp into an under-stairs cupboard packed with boxes, brushes and other household bric-a-brac. The cupboard became a raging inferno in seconds, sending flames leaping up the side of the staircase.

He hurried out the back, picked up his haversack, and moved swiftly around to the front of the house, his gun at the ready.

The driver of the police car saw smoke and flames flickering through gaps in the front door frame. Leaving the police car unlocked and the keys in the ignition, he hurried up the front path and hammered on the front door.

The Dutchman ran past him and, jumping in the police car, drove off like a madman. He swerved to a halt by the steps of The Angel public house with a squeal of brakes. Leaving the engine running and the headlights on, he grabbed his haversack and took off down the steps to the *Black Rose*.

He looked out across the river, wreathed with layers of thin fog with twinkling lights breaking through. There were no other boats in sight. He unhitched the mooring rope, jumped aboard, and started the engines that with a throaty roar sprang to life. He eased back the throttle and the launch lurched forward, scraping down the side of one of the barges until it was clear. He pulled back on the throttle and headed for midstream, leaving a boiling wake.

6

Mr. Budd coughed and spluttered. The room was filling with smoke, and he was trying to think of a way all three of them could elevate themselves high enough to reach the shutter bolts, enabling them to open the shutters and break out through the window — though how they would manage it shackled together, he couldn't imagine.

'We have to get these cuffs off,' he grunted desperately.

'I've got a key,' said Leek.

The big man glared at his sergeant in amazement.

'Why didn't you say so?' he growled. 'Where is it?'

'It's in the pocket of me coat,' answered the sergeant despondently, getting down on his knees again and bending his arms back in an attempt to reach his pocket. The others tried to position themselves to help, but it proved impossible for him to reach the pocket.

'You try to reach it, Peters,' ordered Mr. Budd impatiently.

Peters contorted his body to get his hands in the right position to access the sergeant's pocket. He managed to touch the cold metal of the key with the tip of his fingers but couldn't quite get a grip on it.

'This is intolerable,' said Mr. Budd, feeling the sweat run down his face. 'Tear it — rip out the pocket so the key falls out.'

Peters got a grip on the top of the pocket and gave it a good yank, but the stitching was strong thread and the pocket stubbornly refused to tear.

'Try again,' insisted the big man desperately, sweating profusely as he eyed the flames licking beneath the door, 'or we'll get roasted.'

Outside in the front garden, the police driver heaved a large lump of stone at the window. The glass shattered and sharp-edged pieces fell to the ground. He picked up the stone and used it to break off jagged pieces of glass that remained in the frame. Then he set to work using the stone to batter the middle shutter. It gave at the bottom, but he could see it was still securely fastened at the top. He pushed the shutter inwards with all his strength and was rewarded with a splintering sound as the wooden frame began to break. Encouraged, he tried again. This time it gave way and he was able to peer into the smoke-filled room. The door was turning black, with smoke and flames curling underneath; and the three faces that turned to him were desperate.

'Quick man, climb in and help us get out of these cuffs,' instructed Mr. Budd, his eyes smarting. 'Leek's got a key but we can't reach it.'

'It's in my coat pocket,' explained Leek, coughing. 'The top one.'

The driver scrambled over the sill and quickly located the key. He undid Leek's cuffs and then freed Mr. Budd and Sergeant Peters. They rubbed their wrists with relief as they heard the sound of a fire engine approaching.

'Can someone untie me wrists?' yelled

Leek, backing away from the heat towards the window.

Peters worked on the knotted rope that bound Leek's wrists together while the driver struggled to assist Mr. Budd to escape out of the window, which was not an easy task. After several attempts, he managed it. Mr. Budd tumbled spluttering into the front garden, narrowly avoiding dangerous pieces of broken glass that lay scattered about, each one reflecting flickering flame.

Peters managed to get Leek free. Coughing and spluttering, their lungs full of smoke, they leapt for the window as the door gave way. A searing heat rushed into the room, and the two policemen were just in time to escape an oven in which they would have been burned alive. Leek tumbled through the window opening first, with Peters on his heels. They staggered into the front garden, gulping in wonderful cold air.

A fire engine screeched to a halt outside. Firemen began busily reeling out hoses as a local police car drew up with a screech of brakes. A local inspector and a sergeant leapt out and went up to Mr. Budd, who showed them his credentials and explained briefly what had happened.

'Keep a guard on this place until mornin',' the big man ordered. 'By then things will have cooled down a bit. The house won't survive this fire, but the garden shed should be all right. Don't allow anyone inside the shed until the fingerprint team have completed their work.'

The inspector informed him a black Wolseley had been found with the engine running a hundred yards away outside The Angel, and a constable was guarding it. Mr. Budd dispatched his driver to fetch it.

'There are steps that lead down to a mooring,' the inspector explained.

Mr. Budd nodded. 'This Dutchman feller is loose on the river,' he said, looking shaken as he wiped the sweat from his face with a handkerchief. 'Put a call out to the perlice at the Surrey Docks and Port o' London Authority to double check everyone boarding a cargo boat called the *Gelderland*. Tell them to particularly look out for a Dutchman with a scar running down the left side of his face from the corner of his eye to his jaw. If he tries to escape on the *Gelderland*, we'll nab 'im.'

He considered returning to Scotland Yard; but if the Dutchman had taken to the river, the action would be run from Wapping Operations room, and he wanted to be on hand when the Dutchman was apprehended. When his driver arrived back with the Wolseley, Mr. Budd instructed him to take them to Wapping, before returning Peters to Scotland Yard.

★ ★ ★

While Bentley was reporting to Detective Inspector Telford, Mike Larkin gave Glenda a helping hand onto the duty boat.

'First time out of the office and you're involved with a possible murder and arson. Not bad for a desk woman,' Larkin said to her with a grin.

They watched the firemen battling to

put out the fire that raged out of control within the Natural Art Studios warehouse.

'I felt powerless watching the Dutchman get away,' Glenda told him, clenching her small fists. 'That's what makes me so angry.'

'You don't want to go up against a man with a gun,' Larkin advised. 'A dangerous devil like that. No one expects you to take your duties that seriously, especially after what happened.' He shook his head regretfully. 'I was very sorry to hear about your Dad, Glenda. It was a rotten thing to have happened. I can't imagine how you must be feeling, but I want you to know that I admire you for the way you're handling it.' He squeezed her hand. 'Your courage is an inspiration to us all.'

'Thank you, Mike. That's very kind of you,' she replied, moved but a little embarrassed at the compliment.

'Let go aft,' Reeves shouted to constable Potts as he freed the for'ard rope. 'All ready?' he checked with Larkin, scrambling back into the cabin. 'It's a short run back to Wapping,' he told

Glenda. 'Then you can warm up with a hot drink from the canteen. I expect you'd benefit from a well-earned rest.'

'I won't rest until all the men responsible are brought to justice,' she vowed with a steely determination.

Bentley finished speaking and put down the microphone. 'Explaining all that to Telford was quite a marathon,' he told them.

Larkin was skilfully steering the duty boat through the lock gates at the entrance to St. Katherine's Dock and navigating along the short channel that led onto the river. When they got into midstream, a patch of fog lifted, and Glenda spotted a glow in the sky from the opposite bank.

'That looks like another fire?' she said.

'Looks like a fire, doesn't it?' answered Reeves. 'Something's ablaze right enough, somewhere behind The Angel.'

She was looking back at the glow in the sky from the fire, now moving behind them as they went down river, when she spotted a dark blur approaching fast on their starboard side. Sergeant Reeves had also seen the fast-moving shape.

'There's a launch without lights,' he alerted Larkin, 'coming up on our starboard side.'

Larkin switched on the searchlight, and patches of swirling fog were caught in the beam, writhing like smoke.

'That's the Dutchman!' Glenda warned, shouting above the noise of the engine.

They felt the buffeting from the wash of the powerful launch as it overtook them too close for comfort. The searchlight momentarily picked out a figure at the wheel before it swept along the sleek lines of the *Black Rose*.

Larkin activated the flashing blue police light and opened up the throttle in pursuit. They surged forward, but it soon became evident the duty boat was no match for the powerful engines of the *Black Rose*, and they soon began to lag behind.

As the Dutchman passed by the duty boat with a smirk, travelling at speed towards the Surrey Docks, he was momentarily blinded as the police searchlight caught him full in the face — but not for long.

The throbbing six-cylinder engines quickly propelled him out of range. He checked the fuel gauge and was satisfied to note there was plenty of fuel left for what he planned to do.

Glenda watched the powerful launch accelerate into the foggy distance with a sinking heart, frustrated once again by the Dutchman's escape, but excited to be part of the action for a change instead of sitting at a desk in the control room at Wapping.

'He's getting away, Joe,' she told Bentley urgently through gritted teeth.

'There's not a lot we can do; we're going flat out as it is,' said Bentley, equally frustrated.

Sergeant Reeves grabbed the microphone. 'Thames D4 to TDH — come in please — over.'

'TDH to Thames D4 — TDH to Thames D4 — what is your position? — over.'

'Limehouse,' answered Reeves. 'Proceeding downriver towards the Surrey Docks — speed approximately fifteen knots, in pursuit of a black launch — no navigation lights — estimated speed twenty-five knots, heading downriver. Believed to be steered by wanted fugitive — the Dutchman — armed and dangerous — over.'

'TDH to Thames D4 — alerting all boats to intercept and block launch further down river — over and out.'

The Dutchman knew he couldn't continue downriver without lights at his present speed for very long. The river police would block his way further downstream or the duty boat would catch up with him if he slowed down; it was only a matter of time before a major confrontation. The *Gelderland* must already be leaving the Surrey Docks on the ebb tide; it was time to cut and run. But first he had something else he had to do — a most important move to make, which would allow him to leave the river without being seen.

It was annoying bumping into that duty boat. His eyes went cold and his lips set in a grim line as he throttled down the engines, deliberately allowing the duty boat to catch up on his starboard side.

'He's slowing down,' Larkin warned with a puzzled expression.

'Maybe he's running out of fuel,' suggested Reeves hopefully, training the spotlight on the back of the Dutchman's boat as they approached.

'It's possible,' admitted Larkin, 'but if he was low on fuel, I doubt he would have taken the boat in the first place.'

'I think he's deliberately letting us catch up with him,' warned Bentley. 'We ought to be careful.'

The Dutchman took out his automatic and, swivelling round on his chair, aimed for the searchlight on the police boat. He fired four shots in rapid succession, one of them hitting their target. With a splintering of glass, the searchlight went out. He waited a few moments for his eyes to adjust to the dark until he could make out the outline of the steersman. Then he took careful aim and fired two shots.

The windscreen of the duty boat cracked. Several shards of glass broke free, narrowly missing the crew and shattering into smaller pieces as they crashed onto the cabin floor. Larkin fell back with a curse, his hands slipping from the wheel as he slid sideways off his chair. He felt an intense pain in his head before blacking out.

'Keep down!' yelled Reeves to the others.

He grabbed Larkin and gently lowered him to the floor before scrambling to grab the wheel. The boat was veering off to starboard, bouncing up and down as it cut through the wake from the Dutchman's launch. His hair was swept back and his eyes smarted with the ice-cold air with no windscreen for protection.

Glenda rushed over to Larkin, who lay on the deck unconscious, bleeding profusely from a head wound. She kicked bits of broken glass aside and, kneeling down, carried out a brief examination to assess the damage. A bullet had gouged out a deep channel in the side of his head.

Bentley scrambled to open the first aid kit and, finding a bandage, removed the wrapping and handed it to her. 'This'll have to do for now,' he said.

'Our priority is to get him back to

base,' said Reeves, wrapping his hand in a rag and punching out the remaining shards of glass from the windscreen. 'You take over,' he instructed Bentley as he grabbed the microphone and spoke urgently: 'Thames D4 to TDH — request immediate assistance all available boats — we are pursuing a black launch — estimated speed twenty-five knots — heading downriver with no navigation lights — wanted fugitive fired six shots at us — Constable Larkin wounded in the head — ambulance to stand by — over.'

'TDH to Thames D4 — what is your position? — over.'

'Approaching Greenwich Reach.'

'TDH to Thames D4 — do not attempt to engage launch — return to base — transmission over.'

The Dutchman allowed himself a grim smile as he saw the mayhem he'd caused in the cabin of the duty boat. Ahead, on his starboard side, was the entrance to the Surrey Docks, and moving slowly into midstream across his path was the bulk of the *Gelderland*.

Swivelling around to the port side, the

Dutchman turned his attention back to the Duty Boat and, in particular, the side window of the cabin. He aimed at Joe Bentley and fired, seeing the glass shatter with satisfaction.

The bullet missed Bentley, embedding itself in the hand-held microphone with enough force to rip the microphone out of Reeves's hand and fling it backwards to strike the woodwork. It bounced off, dangling uselessly on its flexible cable.

The Dutchman couldn't find a clear target, but fired two more shots at the commotion inside the cabin. Bentley steered sharply to port, keeping his head down. The bullets went wide. The Dutchman found the full clip he had taken from his bedroom drawer and reloaded.

The *Gelderland* loomed big in the windscreen. The Dutchman expertly swung the wheel of his powerful boat and passed down the starboard side of the cargo ship, opening up the throttle. He'd given the duty boat plenty to keep them occupied, it was time to disappear.

'Damn, we've lost him!' cursed Bentley,

unable to manoeuvre in time to give chase. They were on the port side of the *Gelderland*, with the bulk of the ship between them and the Dutchman's launch. 'Without weapons, there's not much we could do if we managed to apprehend him except get ourselves shot. We can't stop armed criminals!'

'In the old days, our chaps used to wear a sword,' said Reeves.

'Not much good against an automatic,' Bentley joked.

'How's Larkin, Glenda?' asked the sergeant.

'He's still unconscious,' reported Glenda, alarmed to see blood soaking through the bandage she'd just put around the injured man's head. 'We urgently need to get him to hospital.'

'We're on our way back right now,' Reeves told her.

Bentley turned the duty boat through one hundred and eighty degrees, cutting across the wake of the *Gelderland* and headed up river to Wapping.

The Dutchman peered into the misty waters ahead and saw what he was looking for — the dark and deserted entrance to the River Lea and Bow Creek. He was thankful the tide was high. Spinning the wheel, he entered the tributary and steered in the direction of Canning Town.

The launch was of no use to him now, and he looked for somewhere to moor up so he could disembark. He saw a rusty scrap metal barge ahead and tied up to that. Grabbing his knapsack, he climbed an iron ladder up to a yard. It was pitch dark and he couldn't see where he was going, bumping into a rusty old fence that barred his way. He followed the fence, which divided the yard from the river, until he came to a corner from where a narrow track led from the river to the street.

Somewhere in the yard, a dog began barking.

As he reached the street, the barking stopped as suddenly as it had begun. In the silence he heard a train approaching. He stopped still, pinpointing the direction from which the sound travelled, as the train rumbled over points and began to slow down with a screech of brakes. The sounds panned from his right to his left as the train pulled into Canning Town underground station. He now knew in which direction to head and felt momentarily secure. He was sure no one had seen him enter the River Lea. It would take a while before the police located the launch — hopefully not until daylight, by which time he would be far away.

* * *

The group assembled in the canteen at Wapping, sipping mugs of hot steaming coffee, were all in one way or another recovering from shock encounters with the Dutchman. Mike Larkin, shot in the line of duty, was not present; he was recovering in hospital.

'That devil is like an eel the way he keeps slippin' through our fingers,' remarked Mr. Budd irritably after he had listened to their first-hand accounts of the Dutchman's behaviour on the river. He looked enquiringly at the group of experienced river men. 'Where could he have gone?'

'We've lost him,' admitted Inspector Telford ruefully. 'He's disappeared between the Surrey Docks and Greenwich. We had a patrol boat at Greenwich waiting for him but he never showed up.'

'Very inconsiderate of 'im,' grunted Mr. Budd. 'A very dangerous man, Mr. Peter Van der Horst — he's out of control, shooting at perlice like he was at one of those fairground shootin' galleries. We can charge 'im for arson and attempted murder at the very least.'

'Constable Larkin is lucky to be alive,' said Telford. 'I'm pleased to report he's recovered consciousness and is in a stable condition.'

'We need to catch this man,' Superintendent Ramsay emphasised. 'He can't have just disappeared.'

'Between here and Greenwich, there's one place I think he could have gone, and that's Bow Creek,' Glenda suggested. 'If I was him, I'd know that after shooting at us the river was no place to be. I'd ditch the launch, reckoning my chances of escape would be a lot better on dry land. If he ditched his boat at Bow Creek, there's an Underground station nearby.'

'Canning Town,' interrupted Ramsay.

'If I were him, I'd make for that,' finished Glenda. 'I bet he's on the Underground.'

Mr. Budd half opened his eyes; he saw sense in her reasoning. 'Do you have a patrol boat in that area?' he asked Telford.

'The duty boat at Greenwich should remain on patrol in the vicinity in case he attempts to break through,' Telford said as he made for the door. 'I'll arrange for another duty boat to take a look at Bow Creek.'

'If he's escaped onto the Underground, he could go anywhere,' murmured Mr. Budd. 'I'd give a lot to know where he's headed next.'

A few moments later, news came through that the Dutchman's launch had been found where Glenda had predicted, tethered to an old barge in Bow Creek on the Canning Town side. A second report followed close on its heels, confirming a man at the ticket office at Canning Town underground remembered selling a ticket to an unpleasant-looking customer who had been rude to him. He said the man was scary-looking, with a scar down the left side of his face and cold black eyes. He'd been impatient and in a hurry.

'You were right on both counts, Miss Lane,' congratulated Mr. Budd. 'Maybe you should have my job.'

Glenda rewarded the superintendent's compliment with a warm smile. Out of the corner of her eye, she could see Joe Bentley was looking at her like the cat that got the cream. She felt her heart beat quicken as she blushed.

'I'd like to get me hands on that Dutchman,' cried Leek with uncharacteristic venom. 'He put a sack over my head!'

Mr. Budd was about to make a caustic remark, but mindful of the unpleasant experience his sergeant had been put through, thought better of it and instead thrust a hand into a pocket and produced one of his evil-smelling black cigars.

'We must be getting back to the Yard,' he announced with a meaningful look at

Leek. 'I've had quite enough trouble for one day.'

Little did Mr. Budd realise the longest day of his life had barely begun.

7

'You look dog tired,' Bentley said protectively as Glenda yawned and rubbed her eyes. 'You've suffered enough already.'

'It has been a quite dreadful day,' she admitted.

'Let me take you home,' he offered.

Glenda smiled and shook her head. 'I appreciate your kindness, Joe, but I'd prefer to walk. I want to be alone for a while.' Seeing the consternation on his face, she gently touched his arm. 'Don't worry, I'll be all right.'

Bentley felt disappointed but understood she needed time to heal. He went over to a desk, grabbed a pen and a scrap of paper, and scribbled down a number. He pressed the piece of paper into her hand. 'Call me if things get bad.'

She looked at the telephone number and gave him a grateful smile. 'Thank you. I promise I will.'

She put on her coat and tied a dark blue scarf around her head, hiding as much of her face as she could without looking odd. Pulling on her gloves and picking up her shoulder bag, she walked purposefully along Wapping High Street, and was lucky that after a short while she managed to hail a cab.

'Where to, miss?' asked the cabby.

'Number 14 Brady Street, off the Whitechapel Road,' she answered, relaxing back in the leather seat. She no longer felt tired, but was alert, like an animal hunting for food that had caught the scent of its prey. Her destination was a three-storey rundown building next to a bomb site. As the cab drew up outside, she climbed out, paid the cabby and watched it drive off. She paused outside the building, looking up at the grimy sash windows. From her shoulder bag she took out a key ring with two keys on it that her father had given her. Selecting one, she let herself in and switched on the hall light, a single naked bulb of low wattage that produced sufficient illumination to reveal the interior of the building was wholly uninviting and in desperate need of refurbishment. The hall was cold, damp and smelled of dustbins. She climbed the stairs to the first floor, where selecting the second key, she opened a door with the number three on it.

She entered a room that was as drab and inhospitable as the hallway. There was a threadbare carpet on which stood cheap post-war furniture, including a metal-framed bed. She switched on the ceiling light and a small light on the bedside table, finding neither did much to cheer the place up, but revealed a damp patch in one corner by the window.

As she looked around the room, tears filled her eyes as it hit home that her father had spent his last days in this horrid little place. No one in their right mind would want to stay in a room like this out of choice. He had confided to her that he was close to breaking open a big case, but links in the chain were still missing. When he'd found them, he was looking forward to coming home for a while and maybe taking a short break. He never discussed his work in detail or gave her information that might put her in harm's way, which was why he had made her promise never to visit this room except in the event of his death.

Now she was here, she had no idea what to look for. She locked the door and put the key down carefully on the bedside table. She eyed the two drawers of the bedside table and chose to examine them first. The top drawer had fifteen pounds in used notes and an assortment of loose change. There were some keys she recognised as belonging to their house. She didn't want to leave them lying around and put them in her shoulder bag. There were some betting slips, a half-burned candle, a small tin of mints she knew he liked, a packet of Woodbines and a box of matches. Shivering with cold, she grabbed the matches and lit the gas fire.

She slid out the drawer and looked underneath to see if there was anything taped to it. Bending down, she peered inside the cabinet but couldn't spot anything unusual. She repeated the process with the second drawer, which didn't yield anything of significance either, except a large folded street map of central London and a second map detailing the London docks. Both had multiple folds and had been repeatedly used. She sat on the bed and opened them up.

A chest of drawers yielded only clothes and a variety of caps and hats. Piled up on the floor next to it were several telephone directories. A wardrobe contained a suit, a couple of jackets, several pairs of trousers, and an assortment of shoes, all of varying styles and quality, no doubt enabling him to blend in at all levels of society.

She stood in front of the gas fire in an attempt to get warm, but the cold had penetrated right through to her bones. What had she expected to find, a diary with the last weeks of his life neatly annotated?

Then she noticed on the bedside table a grubby dog-eared thriller looking as if it had been read many times. She picked it up and casually turned to the opening chapter, which was called 'The House on the Moor'.

'The house stood on the fringe of a wide expanse of undulating moorland — had stood there in its setting of trees for centuries . . . '

She smiled, thinking of her father lying on the bed reading it, and was overcome by a terrible feeling of loss which she forced herself to fight off. Idly turning the pages until she came to the fourth chapter, which finished a quarter of the way down the page, she felt a tingle of excitement as she saw the rest of the page was filled with her father's thin spidery writing, and brought the book closer to the light. There were two columns of what appeared to be reference numbers, each number followed by a sum of money, the total nearly a million pounds. Beneath the columns was scrawled 'F & F Lombard St'. Thinking this might be part of her father's investigation, she quickly went through the book page by page on the off chance there were other jottings, but found nothing more and put the book in her shoulder bag. Picking up the map of

London, she searched for Lombard Street and discovered it ran from Fenchurch Street to Bank Station right in the heart of the city. She tucked the maps away in her bag and was wondering what to do next when she heard a sound from below. It was the front door to the building closing.

She turned off the lights, plunging the room into darkness except for the glow of the gas fire, and crossed over to the door to listen. She heard something metallic, followed by the unmistakable sound of heavy footsteps ascending the stairs, her ears decoding every footstep until they reached the upper hallway, where they paused for a moment. Then the footsteps approached the door, behind which she stood where they paused again. Thank God she'd had the presence of mind to lock the door.

There was a scuffling noise followed by a faint metallic sound. To her horror, a key turned in the lock.

She sprang backwards into the room as the door began to open, revealing an immense figure filling the doorway and almost blocking out the meagre light from the landing.

'Miss Lane?' said a sleepy voice as Mr. Budd stepped into the room and stood surveying her through half-closed eyes.

'Superintendent Budd,' she acknowledged, letting out a huge sigh of relief as she recognised who it was.

'I apologise if I alarmed you,' he said, walking towards the warmth of the gas fire. 'Why are you here, Miss Lane?'

Glenda looked wistful. 'I've just lost my father, Superintendent, and I wanted to spend a little time with him — where my father spent his last days. I seldom saw him recently, let alone knew what he was getting involved with.'

Of course the real reason she was there was more complicated than she had told Mr. Budd. She was distancing herself from the pain of loss that she knew she would have to face sometime soon, but in the meantime she needed answers just like Mr. Budd needed them, even if for a different reason. He was required to close a case, and she needed closure, and understood that wouldn't happen until she knew everything there was to know about her father's death — a complete picture with no detail left out.

'Can I ask you a question, sir?' she ventured.

'You can ask, Miss Lane, but I can't promise to give yer an answer,' replied the detective evasively, enjoying the warmth that was rising up his back from the gas fire. 'Go ahead, I'll do me best.'

'Why was my father rowing a boat on the river in the dark at that time of the morning? I've thought about it a lot since — since he was found. I keep thinking about it, over and over, and it doesn't make any sense.'

Mr. Budd nodded his head slowly. 'It was a very interestin' and peculiar incident altogether, Miss Lane.'

'Do *you* have an explanation?'

'I have a glimmer of understandin',' Mr. Budd answered cryptically. 'I'll know more tomorrow.'

'What was he doing there?' Glenda persisted, her eyebrows drawn down into a frown.

'I'd rather not speculate. Let me

marshal me facts together, and I promise you'll be the first to know.'

'How did you know I was here, sir?'

'That I *can* answer. This house has been under twenty-four hour surveillance since this morning, in case someone showed up.'

'You mean me?' she said in surprise. 'I've shown up.'

'So you did, so you did,' replied Mr. Budd placidly. 'Did you find anything of interest?'

Glenda squirmed. 'Anything of interest?' she repeated, doing her best to appear vague.

'When you 'ad a look around?' he asked, his eyes narrowing.

'I can't imagine finding anything of interest in this horrid little room.'

'What we imagine and what actually 'appens are often two entirely different things, Miss Lane,' murmured Mr. Budd in his deceptively sleepy voice. 'For example, you may imagine you're a detective pursuing those villains your father was after, dealing out a bit of home-grown justice, only to find yourself completely out of your depth — and instead of you comin' after the villains, them villains come after you. There are a lot of unsavoury characters roaming the streets, and they'd best be handled in an orderly fashion or else you can get bitten. Many of 'em have a nasty bite, very nasty indeed if you get my meanin'. Both of us have experienced that today, 'aven't we?'

She nodded, shaken by the depth of Mr. Budd's perception. 'I'll do my best to remember that advice, sir.'

Glenda had no intention of going home until she had visited Lombard Street.

'Let me run you back to Stepney,' offered Mr. Budd, as if continuing to read her mind.

'I couldn't possibly put you to all that bother, sir,' she replied in her sweetest voice. 'You must have a million more important things to do.'

Mr. Budd sighed. 'I do have a lot on my plate, there's no denying that, but nothing that's as important to me as your good health and wellbeing, Miss Lane. That'd be the first of my priorities.'

'If you drop me off near the Monument on your way back to Scotland Yard, that would be very helpful,' she said.

Mr. Budd looked at her suspiciously. 'Yer planning to commemorate the Great Fire of London, are yer?'

She made a pretence of looking at her watch. 'I thought I'd pay a friend a visit,' she answered unconvincingly.

As they travelled towards the city in the unmarked police car, they discussed their experiences that day, culminating in Mr. Budd issuing a friendly warning.

'Miss Lane, until those unsavoury villains I was talkin' about earlier are safely under lock and key, I get nervous at the idea of you wanderin' the streets of London without protection. You could be in considerable danger.'

'Please don't worry, Superintendent,' she replied, trying to allay his fears. 'I promise I'll get a taxi home.'

Mr. Budd was not convinced. He'd interviewed enough suspects in his time to know instinctively when someone was deviating from the truth.

As the police car drew up to the curb in

Gracechurch Street, close to the Monument, she thanked him for giving her a lift; but as she climbed out of the car, he leaned anxiously towards her.

'If you've got any information, you'd be wise to tell me, Miss Lane.'

'I shall be sure to remember that, sir,' she promised.

She realised there was a lot of sense in the warning Mr. Budd had given her and was fully aware she was being foolhardy, knowing any caution she might have possessed was overridden by a stronger need — the need to know more. She watched the police car pull away and join the city traffic and then she crossed the road, walking purposefully up Gracechurch until she came to the narrow entrance to Lombard Street.

★ ★ ★

Mr. Joseph Fisk was managing director of Fisk and Fossett, a bank founded in 1880 by his grandfather Ebenezer Fisk and an American investor, Henry Fossett. It was an establishment whose name was a synonym for respectability, boasting a long list of discerning clients. Mr. Fisk enjoyed dining out at the best restaurants and visiting the top shows. He lived at Bellevue House, situated on the riverfront at Chiswick.

Fisk closed up the bank, carefully checking no staff remained on the premises, before proceeding with a strategy that had introduced almost two million counterfeit bank notes into general circulation over the past six months. He unlocked a cupboard in his office on the top floor and took out two heavy canvas bags. He carried the bags, one at a time on account of their weight, from his office to the lift and descended four floors to the basement. Opening the lift gate, he hauled out the bags and, stepping over to the vault, expertly entered the combination numbers. He selected one of two keys from a chain secured from a belt around his waist, carefully inserted it in the well-oiled lock, and turned it. Hearing to his satisfaction the bolts withdraw, he grasped a handle and swung back the heavy vault door.

Two of the vault walls were lined with wooden shelves on which were neatly stacked bundles of one- and five-pound notes that had been delivered that morning from the Bank of England. A large steel cabinet stood against the back wall. He inserted his other key in the door of the cabinet and swung open the two doors, revealing banknotes stacked from top to bottom, some in boxes and others in canvas bags like the ones he had brought down from his office. All of the money accumulated in the cabinet was real and had already been painstakingly exchanged for counterfeit.

Turning his attention to that morning's delivery from the Bank of England, he took the packs of real five-pound notes from the wooden shelves around the vault and stacked them in the steel cupboard, replacing them as he went with a bundle of counterfeits from the canvas bags — £190,000 in total. No one would notice they were not the same, because they looked identical except for the serial numbers, which had already been logged and entered in the ledger by his manager

Henry Apple. There was no reason for Henry to check the serial numbers a second time.

In the days ahead, the counterfeit notes would find their way to various outlets — payouts to customers, wage rolls, shops and institutions. The real banknotes, once liberated from the cupboard in the vault, would be put to use building a huge property portfolio and bolstering the bank's profits by being paid back into the bank as fake interest received and invented loans repaid. The huge cash balance left over after these transactions was divided up as the cash spoils of the operation, with the property portfolio as a future investment. To date, the operation had worked very success-fully, but couldn't continue to do so as the special paper the counterfeit notes were printed on had ran out. There were more than sufficient spoils to keep the gang in luxury for the rest of their lives. It was time to shut up shop.

Fisk closed the vault and returned in the lift to his office on the top floor where, he worked steadily on his secret parallel accounts for a while. He was on the point of going home when the staff entrance bell rang. He spoke into the intercom: 'Yes?'

'It's Peter,' announced the Dutchman.

'What are you doing here, Van der Horst?' Joseph demanded, horrified the Dutchman had visited the bank in person. 'I expressly forbade — '

The Dutchman interrupted curtly, 'Never mind all that. This is urgent. Let me in.'

Fisk sensed trouble. Sheltered from a world war and brought up in relative security, he had always tried to avoid it. He took the lift down to the ground floor and reluctantly opened the rear staff door to the bank. The Dutchman pushed roughly past him and headed towards the open lift, carrying his haversack.

'Take me to the vault,' he demanded.

Joseph Fisk was aghast. He had never let anyone into the vault except himself and his Henry Apple. 'The vault?' he repeated, his jaw dropping with shock.

'Yes, the vault, Joseph,' repeated the Dutchman impatiently. 'Be quick! I have some cash to keep safe and I don't have much time.'

Fisk looked at him suspiciously. 'Cash.'

The Dutchman cut him off gruffly as he entered the lift, kicking his haversack as a portent of violence. 'I can't go into long explanations right now; I'm in a hurry.'

Fisk hesitated, unsure how to stand his ground. He didn't want a row with the Dutchman, whom he feared more than anyone he had ever met; but he also had no intention of letting him anywhere near his vault. He knew something fishy was going on, and the Dutchman had other reasons to gain access to the vault than depositing a haversack full of cash. His suspicion was immediately proved right as the Dutchman produced his automatic and levelled it at the banker.

'The first shot will be in your left leg,' he threatened in a cold voice, 'and the second your other leg. Don't test me.'

Fisk was not a violent man and broke out in a cold sweat of fear. He had no doubt the Dutchman would carry out his threat, and he capitulated at once, entering the lift and pressing the 'Basement' button. He went through the procedure of opening the vault, playing along while trying hard to think of a way out of his predicament.

The Dutchman pushed him roughly inside once the vault door stood open. 'Now open the cabinet,' he instructed.

Fisk hesitated, in no doubt now of the Dutchman's intentions. He'd come to rob him. The Dutchman's eyes glittered with anger at the banker's hesitation.

He fired twice.

Fisk gave a small gasp of pain as he crumpled to the vault floor, his body twisted in a grotesque position. For a moment he looked at the Dutchman uncomprehendingly, and then he died, his lifeless eyes staring up at the ceiling.

The Dutchman picked up the two spent cartridges and slipped them into his pocket. Swiftly he unclipped the chain from Fisk's belt and selected the key that opened the steel cabinet at the back of the vault. He inserted the key in the lock and, opening the cabinet doors, greedily surveyed the shelves stacked with boxes of genuine banknotes. He needed transport, and searched through the dead banker's pockets for the keys to his Daimler. He didn't find them, but had a good idea where they would be.

He took the lift to Fisk's office on the top floor. He saw Fisk's coat hanging from a bentwood coat stand and found the banker's car keys in one of the pockets. Forgetting to turn off the light, he went back to the lift and took it to the ground floor. He let himself out by the staff door and walked through Change Alley to Cornhill, where he knew the banker parked his car. He opened the garage doors and climbed into the driver's seat of the Daimler. Starting the engine, he drove the big saloon along Change Alley and parked in a small yard close to the rear entrance to the bank. He turned off the engine, leaving the headlights on so he would be able to see what he was doing.

He began the laborious job of transferring the money from the steel cupboard at the back of the vault to the lift, ignoring the body of Joseph Fisk as if it wasn't there. When the cupboard was bare, he closed the vault door, locked it, and spun the combination, feeling certain the banker's body wouldn't be discovered until the bank opened in the morning, and possibly not even then.

⋆　⋆　⋆

Lombard Street was dimly lit in monochromatic shades of grey, from the deeper doorways to the dark grey rectangles of the unlit windows, the metallic grey of the road surface, the darker grey of the wet pavement, and above a uniform darkening sky. As Glenda Lane didn't want to be noticed, this gloom was helpful; but the lack of illumination also made it difficult to read the names on the buildings.

A short way down Lombard Street, she came to Christopher Wren's St. Edmund, King and Martyr on her right, a church next to a cleared bomb site. Beyond the church there was a turning into Birchin Lane. There was nothing of interest here, and she pressed on until she came to Change Alley, where she paused by a four-storey building, shivering, her cheeks numb with cold. She looked up and down the street, but there wasn't a soul about. She peered up the steps to the entrance. On a brass plate she could just make out:

FISK AND FOSSETT
FOUNDED 1880

She caught her breath and felt her heartbeat quicken. 'F & F Lombard St' — this had to be the place noted by her father in the book. She stepped across the street to get a better look. It was dark except for a single lit window on the top floor. She assumed someone must be working late, long after banking hours. She listened for any unusual sound and searched for any sign of activity. For a full minute, she stood still watching the front of the bank, but it was like staring at a still photograph.

She could hardly ring the bell at this time of night and decided to take a look around the back, which could be reached down Change Alley. The alley was pitch black, forcing her to feel her way down the side of the building until she came to a corner. She couldn't see what lay beyond, and was thinking of returning when it was daylight, when the powerful beams belonging to the headlights of a car approached from a tunnel-like entrance ahead of her. The headlights enabled her to see that the alley opened onto a yard that provided access to the back of the bank and other tall buildings. She glimpsed dustbins and discarded boxes, all in a flash, before she jumped back into the alley and pressed herself to the wall.

A powerful saloon came to a halt not three feet from where she stood, the headlights still full on. She dared not look but heard the engine stop and a door open, followed by the crunch of gravel as someone heavy got out. Footsteps went around the vehicle, and there came to her ears the click of a boot opening. The footsteps went to the building, a door opened, and the footsteps changed pitch as they crossed an interior wooden floor. She faintly heard the whirring noise of the lift motor followed by a metallic rattle as lift gates were pulled open. It was like listening to a play on the radio; she could picture clearly what was happening, though she couldn't see anything.

Pulling her head scarf down onto her forehead, she ventured a peep around the corner of the building. A wedge of light shone out through an open door illuminating a big shiny black saloon with the driver door open and the boot lid up.

'You haven't heard the lift doors close,' a voice in her head reminded her. 'Keep out of sight.'

The footsteps returned as she sprang back into concealment. She expected them to stop at the car, but to her horror they headed directly towards her. She wondered if she'd been seen, and pressed herself to the wall as a tall and menacing shadow of a man, projected by the car headlights, moved across an opposite wall in front of her. It was followed by a dark figure that strode into view, marching purposefully over to the dustbins and cardboard boxes. The flapping coattails and heavy gate told her it was the Dutchman. If he turned around, he couldn't fail to see her.

Something small and sleek darted from the dustbins, scurrying across the small yard and up the alleyway upon the other side. It was a large brown rat the size of a small cat. It had been disturbed by the Dutchman, who paused and briefly stared after it before rummaging through the boxes, selecting those he thought suitable.

Glenda crossed to the opposite wall of the alley so she'd be out of sight as he returned, carrying a couple of empty boxes. Pressing herself into a recess, she froze, not daring to make a sound until she had heard him enter the building. She could hear scuffles and the sound of boxes being dragged across a floor and stacked up. The Dutchman was taking things out of the lift.

She was in two minds as to what to do next. The sensible police procedure would have been to find a telephone box, telephone Scotland Yard, report sighting the Dutchman and give them the number plate of the Daimler. But if she were to leave the scene and go in search of a public call box, the Dutchman might drive off during her absence and a unique opportunity would be lost.

She made up her mind what she would do and, alert for any sign of danger, tiptoed swiftly to the front of the car. She crouched down, taking care her shoulder bag didn't hit anything and make a noise. Her heart was beating loudly and her breathing was erratic; surely the Dutchman would hear her when he returned.

Bent double to avoid being seen above the car windows, she sneaked to the rear passenger door and cautiously lifted her head until she could see into the open doorway of the bank. There was a single light illuminating an expanse of polished floor that went up to an open lift gate. The Dutchman had his back to her, busily sorting through a large pile of boxes and bags he'd removed from the lift.

She knew this might be her only opportunity. Gripping her shoulder bag firmly in her other hand, she opened the rear passenger door, careful to keep her head below window level. She leaned forward and wriggled inside like a human python onto thick carpet, corkscrewing onto her back so that she faced the roof. Lifting her shoulders, she managed to reach the door lever and pull the heavy door closed with the softest click. Then she lay back, rolled onto her side, and pressed her body into the recess where the floor went under the backs of the front seats. Her shoulder bag was a nuisance, but she managed to wedge it into a gap near her head. She closed her eyes and concentrated on keeping motionless and regaining her composure.

With trepidation, she heard the Dutchman's footsteps approach the car and knew, for good or ill, there was no going back. The suspension of the car gave as a heavy box was placed in the boot. Footsteps moved rapidly backwards and forwards from the bank to the car several times as the Dutchman transferred the heavy boxes of cash.

What if there wasn't sufficient space in the boot, so he would have to put some boxes in the passenger compartment? The thought terrified her. She hadn't thought of that possibility before and felt quite ill.

If that were to happen, there wasn't any way she could avoid discovery. She broke out into a cold sweat and wished she was at home tucked up in bed.

Finally, the rear door of the building shut with a bang followed by the rattle of keys. Then she almost jumped out of her skin and gave herself away, as a sudden squeak of leather was loud in her ear. There followed a protest by springs as a heavy body sank into the driver's seat.

The car door slammed shut. A key was turned in the ignition and the engine came to life. The Dutchman's elbow appeared over the back of the driver's seat as he twisted around to look out of the rear window, reversing the big car back along the alley and out onto Cornhill. He was aware he was driving a conspicuous car, but assumed he had all night before the police would be on the lookout for it. There were unlikely to be any problems until the following day, by which time the Daimler would be securely hidden from view and he would be richer by half a million pounds in genuine five-pound notes. He drove the Daimler out of the

City towards Romford.

Stretched out on the carpeted floor in the back of the big saloon, pressed close into the support structure of the front seats, not daring to move, Glenda could see little but street lamps streaking across the rear window. When some dust got up her nose, she held her breath in an attempt not to sneeze, until she could hold it no longer and was forced to slowly fill her lungs with air. Then, after a while, her right leg began to itch until she longed to scratch it. She tried not to think about it, but the irritation grew worse. The itch became an all-consuming nightmare, until she would have given anything to stop it. In acute discomfort, she freed an arm and slid her fingers towards the itch, but her arm wasn't long enough to reach the spot without her bending her leg. She had no doubt that if the Dutchman discovered her, he would end her life immediately, without any scruples. Yet despite this danger, or maybe because of it, she had never before felt so energised and alive.

To her immense relief, the Dutchman

turned onto a lesser road that was not a smooth one, so that any small movements she made were masked by the saloon's contact with the rough surface. She bent her leg, managed to reach the itching spot, and scratched it vigorously. She smiled with relief as the itch went away.

She was acutely aware of her position, with no idea as to her destination. As time went on, this uncertainty played upon her mind, unsettling her. By the time the big car finally came to a halt and the Dutchman climbed out, she still had no idea where she was, but was just grateful they had arrived somewhere at last. She was back listening to a real life radio drama — the sound of footsteps, a garden gate, a key in a lock, followed by voices.

When she tried to move, it was painful; her legs had become stiff and cramped, and the circulation had been cut off from one arm, leaving it heavy like a piece of dead meat. She massaged it, and slowly life returned in the form of pins and needles as her blood began circulating again.

She discerned two sets of approaching footsteps.

'Why my brother's car?' a foreign-sounding voice was asking.

'I just obey instructions, Isaac,' replied the Dutchman, gruff and belligerent.

The boot was opened, and there followed bumps and scuffles as the cargo was unloaded.

'Must be half a million here,' commented the man called Isaac.

'I didn't stop to count it,' grunted the Dutchman.

They carried all the boxes away and slammed the boot lid shut. The Dutchman climbed back into the car and drove it a short way further on before getting out and leaving the driver's door open, allowing cold air to rush into the warm interior. Glenda heard heavy-duty bolts pulled back, followed by loud scraping and rattling noises that sounded like heavy doors were being dragged across uneven ground.

The Dutchman got back in and drove the car forward a few yards. He applied the handbrake and turned off the engine, but left the headlights on as a source of light. Through the car window, Glenda could just make out the timber construction of a barn.

Her eyes wide and staring, she listened on full alert, knowing the Dutchman must be sitting in the front seat but wasn't moving, and it would have been easy to forget he was still there. Then there came the squeak of leather and the opening of the driver's door, followed by a shoe scraping on the ground and then footsteps. There were several metallic sounds, a match was struck, and Glenda could detect the warm flickering glow of a lantern approaching the car accompanied by footsteps.

The Dutchman put the lantern on the ground. There was creaking leather as he leaned across the front seat of the car, followed by the click of a switch as he turned off the headlights. The car door slammed shut and the footsteps went away, the light from the lantern going with them. There followed scuffles as the Dutchman swung the barn doors shut with a clatter and a bang. Bolts were rammed home.

Glenda was left alone in the pitch black; there was not the faintest glimpse of light anywhere. She rolled away from the front seats and rested on the back seat of the Daimler for several seconds while she recovered. Then, reaching for her shoulder bag, she opened the passenger door and climbed out. Carefully closing the door behind her, she felt her way along the side of the car until she came to the warm bonnet. With her arms outstretched, she continued forward, counting her footsteps like a blind person, until after twelve steps she came up against wood — the barn doors. She pushed and was rewarded with movement, accompanied by a slight rattle. She shifted to her right, feeling her way to where the two doors joined. She slid the flat of her hand upwards against the rough wood until she found the cold steel of a bolt, which she withdrew. Then downwards — she withdrew the floor bolt. With a hard shove, she allowed the barn doors to swing open, just sufficiently for her to squeeze through.

It was still night; the sky was overcast with no hint of a moon, countryside dark, bitterly cold and frosty with little in the way of a breeze. The tang of the sea assailed her nostrils, reminding her of when she was a child living near Shinglesea.

What time was it? She looked at her watch but couldn't make out sufficient detail to tell.

Then a splinter of light through gaps in a high hedgerow caught her eye, and she headed toward it, eventually finding a gap through which she could make out the shape of a house that was set back from the lane. She followed the hedge until she arrived at a low gate. The light came from a downstairs window dimly illuminating a round stone well in the front garden. It all looked familiar, and her eyebrows drew together into a deep frown as she realised why.

It wasn't surprising the tang of the sea had reminded her of when she was a child living near Shinglesea, as this *was* Well End near Shinglesea. She was about to enter the garden of the home where she grew up before moving to London, where she was raised as a child in the 1930s. She fought off fond memories of her childhood which immediately invaded her consciousness, while forcing herself to remain in the present as she grappled for an explanation as to why the Dutchman, of all the places he could have driven to, had deliberately chosen this one.

Why had the Dutchman driven to her old home address?

The shocking notion that her father might have been implicated in the counterfeiters' criminal activities hit her hard, and try as she might, she couldn't arrive at any realistic explanation. She was determined to find out the truth. Carefully lifting the latch on the gate, she swung it open.

Avoiding the path, she sought the safety of shrubbery that bordered the front garden on her right, which the light spilling from the window didn't quite reach. She brushed past leaves, blending into the bushes, as she crept closer to the window. She turned her watch face to the light and saw it had just gone one o'clock.

Through the window, she saw an empty kitchen that brought back memories — the warm glow given out by the anthracite stove and a drawing of a black cat with a red bow tie that still hung on the wall. As she was trying to come to terms with what she was seeing, the Dutchman came into view. She snapped back to her present reality with a jolt and could feel a surge of adrenaline coursing through her veins.

He marched past a scrubbed kitchen table to a door she knew led to a pantry. He disappeared out of sight, only to return a few moments later carrying two cans of baked beans and a can opener. He opened both the cans, spooning the contents into a saucepan, which he placed on the hot stove.

He briefly disappeared from view again, going out into the hallway, only to reappear moments later carrying a three-quarters-full bottle of whisky and a glass tumbler. He poured a generous amount of the single malt and took a long draught that almost emptied the glass. With the glass still in his hand, he crossed leisurely to the window and stared out.

Glenda withdrew into the bushes, backing into the foliage until she felt cold frosty leaves wrap themselves around her, providing a sensation of support and security. It seemed impossible that those cold black eyes couldn't see her, but obviously they did not. After what seemed an interminable time, the Dutchman turned away, drained his glass of whisky, and grabbing the saucepan off the stove, slammed it down onto the kitchen table. He began ravenously eating the food straight out of the pan while drinking copious amounts of whisky from the bottle.

Glenda could feel the cold getting into her bones, and was considering her next move when another man came into the kitchen who she assumed must be Isaac. He was swarthy with dark wavy hair and a small beard.

The Dutchman pushed the saucepan away from him and looked up at the man, who began arguing rapidly and gesticulating with short abrupt arm movements that grew increasingly frantic.

She strained to hear what they were saying, but the argument reached her ears as a faint hubbub that was undecipherable. Then she watched as the Dutchman lost his temper, pushed back his chair, and leapt to his feet. He began cursing the other man, who put up his hands as if to ward off a blow. A gun appeared in the Dutchman's hand that spat flame.

With loud reports, two shots rang out.

Glenda stared in horror as the foreign-looking man, his eyes wide with surprise, fell back clutching his chest. He crumpled to the floor out of sight below the sill of the window.

She'd just witnessed a murder!

What should she do? What *could* she do, except get herself shot if she interfered in any way? She stayed where she was and continued watching.

The Dutchman slammed his gun on the table and slumped back into his chair with a look of satisfaction. He grabbed the whisky bottle and took a swig, stretching out his legs and kicking away a chair that was in his way. He stared abstractedly at the body of the man he'd just killed.

Glenda noticed there were only two fingers of whisky left in the bottle and wondered how long it would be before the alcohol took effect.

After what seemed an interminable time, the Dutchman scraped back his chair and stumbled to his feet. He lunged at the whisky bottle and, putting it to his lips, emptied it in one go. Stepping over the body, he staggered into the hall, turning off the kitchen light as he went.

Glenda's cheeks were numb and she could no longer feel her legs and feet. She'd have given half her life savings for a mug of hot chocolate and the other half for a hot bath.

After a while a gable light appeared in what had once been her old bedroom. She presumed the Dutchman was preparing for bed, and had no choice but to wait patiently for the light to go off, when she could put a plan she had been formulating into execution.

8

Superintendent Robert Budd returned to his office at Scotland Yard that evening to find two reports waiting for him — the first from Interpol and the second from the Bank of England, sent over by Frobisher, which he read first.

The report gave details about the paper the forgers had used. It was a precious rag-based paper, specially formulated and watermarked for printing fake banknotes at the behest of the Reich Main Security Service during the war. The paper had been manufactured at a paper mill in Cologne, owned by a Dieter Kretschmann, but the mill no longer existed. Along with much of Cologne's industrial area, the mill had been bombed by the British in July 1943, and reduced to rubble.

Mr. Budd lit one of his black cigars as he contemplated a wartime connection. If the paper had been specially manufactured for the Third Reich and the machinery that manufactured it destroyed, some of the banknote paper had to have survived.

Had Dieter Kretschmann survived the war? If he was still alive, where was he now?

A paper trail might provide the means to uncover the whole story. His mind went back to his discussion in the evidence room at Wapping, when Frobisher had told him the plates used to print the notes had been forged since the war because they were signed by the current chief cashier, Percival Beale, who'd taken over from the previous chief cashier, Kenneth Peppiatt, in 1949. He contemplated the notion that someone with a rare talent had etched the plates in order to print on old paper that had survived a bombing raid. Perhaps a quantity of paper had been shipped somewhere prior to the raid, avoiding destruction, but was never used — a printing works?

Frobisher had also mentioned that the men behind Operation Bernhard had produced the best counterfeit banknotes ever seen — the wartime connection looked promising. The roots of this caper went back to the war, he felt sure of it. However, conjecture was one thing — he needed hard facts as evidence that would hold up in a court of law.

He read the second report from Interpol detailing the survivors of Sachsenhausen. He immediately put a call through to Interpol urgently requesting information on Peter Van der Horst and Dieter Kretschmann and if there was any connection between them.

If the Dutchman acted as a facilitator for getting the freshly printed notes to England, what happened to them after that? How did they get into the pockets of the public? How did they get laundered for real cash? A distributor had to be involved, and the most obvious choice for such a large sum would be a bank, which was why the superintendent had asked Sergeant Leek to draw up a list. He summoned his melancholy sergeant to find out how he'd been getting on.

Leek came into the office clutching a heavy book. 'I've found a directory,' he told his superior, tapping the cover with a thin finger. 'They're all listed in here. I've marked the page.'

'Let me 'ave a look,' said Mr. Budd, grabbing the directory and spreading it open on the desk in front of him. He picked up the Interpol report listing the Sachsenhausen survivors and, aligning it with the page in the directory his sergeant had marked, began comparing them.

'What are you looking for?' asked Leek in an attempt to show interest.

'Anythin' that — ' He broke off, a finger marking an entry halfway down the page. 'Here we are. Fisk and Fossett, a bank in Lombard Street.' He moved his finger to Frobisher's report — and one of the survivors of Sachsenhausen was an Isaac Fisk!

'It could be a coincidence,' said Leek sceptically. 'Probably quite a lot of people have the name Fisk.'

Mr. Budd wasn't listening to him. A number of connections were racing through his brain, the chief being WPC Lane's voice telling him, 'I thought I'd pay a friend a visit.'

He'd had his suspicions about WPC Lane, but now he was sure they'd been correct. The Monument was a short walk from Lombard Street. Glenda Lane knew something, and that was why she'd gone there — something she'd discovered in her father's room in Whitechapel?

The Dutchman had caught an Underground train from Cannon Street, a few stops from the city. His sergeant might be right, and it might all be a coincidence; but what better place to seek shelter when on the run than the safety of a bank with an owner who was related to a master forger from Sachsenhausen?

He grabbed his coat and hat. 'I need to get to Fisk and Fossett right away,' he told Leek. 'I want to speak to Mr. Fisk without a moments delay.'

Leek looked at his watch.

'They'll be closed now,' he said gloomily.

'Find out where he lives,' instructed Mr. Budd impatiently. 'Get him on the telephone and ask him if he's related to the other Fisk, this Isaac feller. If he is, ask him to meet me at his bank. I think Glenda Lane could be in grave danger.'

★　★　★

Sergeant Leek had not been able to make contact with Joseph Fisk. When he'd managed to get through to the banker's residence in Chiswick, his housekeeper was already agitated because he had not returned for dinner, which was most unusual. She was worried something might have happened to him and gave Leek the name and telephone number of the manager of the bank, Mr. Henry Apple.

'Ask Mr. Apple to meet us outside the bank without delay,' Mr. Budd ordered, also alarmed the banker hadn't returned for his dinner.

Matters had moved swiftly but not swiftly enough. As Mr. Budd's police car drew up at the front of Fisk and Fossett, the Dutchman had been backing away from the rear.

Mr. Budd, Sergeant Leek, and a tall military-looking man with short cropped hair representing the City of London police, an Inspector Brand, were grouped outside the bank waiting for the manager to appear. They had found no sign of forced entry but had noticed the light in the room on the top floor.

'I don't like it,' Mr. Budd remarked, feeling his cheeks go numb with cold as he stared up at the face of the building. 'Something's wrong.'

He omitted to say that he also didn't like the fact that he'd found no sign of Glenda Lane upon arrival and, while he'd not expected to see her outside the bank waving a flag, her absence added to his unease. He'd convinced himself she wasn't with any friend but had probably got herself mixed up with whatever had happened at the bank.

'Leek, you'd better take a look around the back for any sign of a forced entry.'

Sergeant Leek produced a torch and entered the dark throat of Change Alley. He returned a few minutes later to report there was a rear staff entrance but it was locked with no sign of the lock having been forced.

Mr. Budd was relieved when Henry Apple arrived. He was turning fifty, bald, stocky, and rather self-important. 'I'm the manager, Mr. Henry Apple. What's this all about?' he demanded.

Mr. Budd showed him his credentials. 'I'm sorry you've had to be dragged out at this hour, sir,' he began apologetically.

'Something about a robbery,' said the manager, looking worried.

'We've checked this entrance,' Mr. Budd told him, jerking his head towards the double doors, 'and around the back. We found no sign of forced entry.'

'What's your reasoning behind suspecting a robbery?' asked Mr. Apple sharply.

The superintendent glanced up. 'There's a light still on up there, on the top floor. Do you have any idea why that might be?'

Henry Apple stood back and followed the big man's gaze. 'That would be Mr. Fisk's office. He often stayed on after the rest of the staff had gone home.'

'Does he make a habit of leaving his light on?'

'Not to my knowledge. Surely you don't expect a robbery has taken place just because someone left a light on?'

Inspector Brand looked at Mr. Budd with interest. He too wondered why he was there.

Mr. Budd had no real answer to this and drew himself to his full height. 'A combination of facts I am unable to disclose,' he bluffed. 'Would you be so kind as to open up the bank to enable us to look around to make certain everythin' is in order?'

Henry Apple went up the steps and fumbled with a bunch of keys. By the annoyed expression on his face, he was not at all content with the superintendent's vague explanation for dragging him out at such a late hour.

Mr. Budd shone his light upon the lock, hoping he wasn't conducting a wild goose chase. The bank manager opened the doors and everyone followed him inside.

Henry Apple turned on the lights and paused, looking around, frowning.

'What's the matter?' asked Mr. Budd.

'The alarm should have come on,' he remarked. 'But it's off. Mr. Fisk would never have left the bank without setting it.'

'It's highly probable Mr. Fisk hasn't left the bank,' commented Mr. Budd, relieved that he might not be on a wild goose chase after all, but very concerned for Mr. Fisk's good health. 'Leek, you go to the top floor and see if anyone's still up there. We'll take a look at the vault.'

'That's in the basement,' said Henry Apple. 'We can take the lift.'

'How do I get to the top floor?' asked Leek.

'You take the stairs,' said Mr. Budd.

'If you go along that corridor,' suggested Mr. Apple, 'you'll come to the staff lift. You can take that to the top floor.'

Leek gave the manager a thin smile of appreciation and set off.

When the others arrived outside the vault, Henry Apple entered the combination and inserted his key. With a rewarding click, the big steel door of the vault swung open to reveal Joseph Fisk lying on the floor in a grotesque position, his sightless eyes staring at the ceiling, and two bullet holes in his chest.

Henry Apple stood rooted to the spot, unable to believe the evidence of his own eyes as he stared at the body in horror, transfixed, unable to comprehend how the owner of the bank could have been murdered and locked in his own vault.

'I was afraid of somethin' like this,' said Mr. Budd with an indrawn breath.

Henry Apple had turned quite pale. As he agitatedly rubbed his bald head, his hands sported a slight tremor. 'This is the most terrible business, Superintendent,' he said when he had regained a little of his composure. 'Most terrible. How can this have happened?'

Mr. Budd nodded sympathetically. 'That's what I'm here to find out, sir,' he said, used to seeing many dead bodies over the years and often forgetting the shocking effect a dead person could have on a live one. 'I realise it's come as quite a shock discovering Mr. Fisk in this way,' he added, glancing at the body on the floor. 'Apart from Mr. Fisk, is there anything out of order? Is there anything missing — cash for example?'

Henry Apple could see that the packets of cash he had taken in from the Bank of England that morning were still stacked on the wooden shelves that lined the vault.

'Everything appears to be as I left it this morning,' he assured the superintendent. 'Except, of course . . . ' He broke off, looking down at his employer.

'Do you check the serial numbers of the cash in the vault?' Mr. Budd intervened hastily.

The bank manager nodded. 'Oh, yes. Every time a consignment of new notes comes in from the Bank of England, I personally log the serial numbers in the ledger.'

'When was the last delivery?'

'This morning.'

'Would you mind fetching the ledger and checking the serial numbers again?' Mr. Budd suggested.

The bank manager looked at him sharply, as if he were being accused of malpractice. 'Are you suggesting — ?'

'I'm not suggesting anything Mr.

Apple,' Mr. Budd went on, frowning heavily. 'I need to make certain of the facts.'

'This looks like an inside job to me,' said Inspector Brand when Henry Apple was out of earshot. 'No sign of forced entry, so whoever opened the vault knew the combination and possessed a key. That narrows it down to the dead owner or the manager.'

'I have no doubt that Mr. Fisk opened up the vault himself and that he was forced to do so by the man who was to rob 'im and murder 'im,' stated the big man, aware that Brand would be handling the investigation as the bank fell within his jurisdiction. 'This is part of a larger counterfeit operation. The notes they produce are of exceptional quality, and I wouldn't be surprised — ' He jerked his head towards the stacks of new banknotes. ' — to find these are substitutions.' He selected a bundle of new notes from a shelf at random and extracted one of the crisp white notes, then held it up to the light to illuminate the watermark. 'Unless I'm much mistaken, these are counterfeit,' he told Brand.

'Do you think Mr. Apple could have anything to do with this, sir?' asked Brand in a low conspiratorial voice.

'It's a possibility,' answered the superintendent with thoughtful consideration. 'But unlikely.'

Mr. Budd made a careful examination of the body and searched the pockets of the clothes the dead banker was wearing. He was hoping to find keys, but there weren't any. He looked around for two spent cartridges, but was unable to find them and assumed the killer had been thorough and picked them up.

Henry Apple returned carrying his ledger and, careful to avoid the dead banker, rested the heavy book on a shelf. He turned the pages to the last entry and began comparing his logged serial numbers to those of the packets on the shelf. He started out with the assumption that double-checking the serial numbers would be a formality, only to begin shaking his head in confusion as he saw the numbers no longer matched. He turned to Mr. Budd and Inspector Brand, who were waiting patiently outside the vault.

'Something *is* very odd here,' he admitted to Mr. Budd with a puzzled frown. 'These aren't the numbers I recorded this morning. I assure you I have no idea how this can have happened.'

'I think the notes you checked this morning fresh from the Bank of England have been removed this evening and replaced with counterfeit ones,' Mr. Budd explained.

Henry Apple, careful to avoid the prone figure of Joseph Fisk, quickly examined several other packets of notes. They didn't match his records either. 'Where are the banknotes I recorded?' he asked.

'They've been stolen, Mr. Apple,' answered Mr. Budd, unable to stifle a yawn. 'I assume they'll be far away from here by now.'

'But who — who could have taken them?' asked the astonished bank manager.

Before Mr. Budd could reply, Inspector

Brand intervened.

'You have to be my prime suspect, Mr. Apple,' he cautioned.

'That is an outrageous assertion, Inspector,' objected Mr. Apple. 'I've served Mr. Fisk with the utmost loyalty for several years, and I can assure you I have nothing to do with this terrible incident, nothing at all. If you care to check with Mrs. Apple, she'll confirm I arrived home at six forty-five this evening, my usual time, and that I've been home all evening, until you called requesting my presence here.'

'Thank you, sir,' replied the Inspector, watching the bank manager's face carefully. 'We will, of course, be taking a statement from Mrs. Apple.'

Mr. Budd thought that unless Mr. Apple was a consummate actor, which his personality suggested he was not, Mr. Apple was telling the truth. He turned his attention to the steel cabinet at the back of the vault, finding it intriguing.

'Unusual to have a locked cabinet inside a vault?' he queried, glancing at the manager. 'What's it for?'

Henry Apple looked as if he'd been caught out, and immediately lost some of his authority by admitting, 'I don't have a key for that cabinet. Mr. Fisk never opened it in my presence, so the truth is, I've never seen inside it. I have no idea when he did open it or how frequently. He told me he kept personal papers in it, and as he was the owner of the bank, I saw no reason to raise the subject again.'

Mr. Budd and Inspector Brand stared at the steel cupboard with anticipation that it might reveal something astounding.

'Mr. Fisk was the only one with a key?' asked Inspector Brand.

'He kept it on his person,' said the manager, 'on a keychain with the key to the vault.'

Mr. Budd rubbed gently at a soft cheek. 'It's not there now,' he said, turning to Inspector Brand. 'Can yer arrange for a locksmith to open the cabinet?'

The inspector looked at his watch and appeared doubtful.

'You might have to wake someone up,'

added Mr. Budd meaningfully.

A photographer arrived and proceeded to cover every angle with a series of blinding flashes. As soon as he had completed his work, a fingerprint team moved in and began dusting the door to the vault and the steel cabinet with a fine silver powder. Henry Apple watched these proceedings with increasing alarm.

'Can Mr. Fisk be covered over with something?' he requested. 'He shouldn't be left lying there like that. It's not dignified.'

'He'll be goin' to the morgue as soon as our people 'ave completed their work,' answered Mr. Budd. 'I'm afraid there's nothing dignified in a murder.'

The word 'murder' triggered in Mr. Apple a sense of panic that nothing at the bank would ever be the same again. 'I don't know what will happen now. Obviously, I'll have to close the bank.'

'Until we've completed our investigations,' admitted Inspector Brand. 'We'll have to determine what's real and what isn't.'

'The publicity,' said Mr. Apple, throwing his hands in the air.

'How long have you worked at the bank, Mr. Apple?' asked Mr. Budd.

'Five years this April,' the manager answered promptly.

'Mr. Fisk has a house in Chiswick?'

Mr. Apple nodded. 'That's correct, a very nice house indeed.'

'How did he get to work?'

'He has a Daimler,' answered Mr. Apple, opening his eyes wide.

'Where is it garaged?' Mr. Budd enquired.

'It must still be here!' the bank manager exclaimed. 'Mr. Fisk keeps it in a garage off Cornhill. You go through the alley at the back of the bank.'

Mr. Budd couldn't hide his impatience. 'Where are the keys? There were no car keys on him.'

Sergeant Leek, who had arrived via the stairs, carrying a coat, overheard him. 'I checked the desk drawers. There were no keys in the room where the light was on,' he reported, holding up a coat. 'I found this.'

'That's Mr. Fisk's coat,' confirmed Henry Apple.

'There's nothing in the pockets,' Leek said. 'I've checked all the other floors and there's no sign of anyone.'

'Is there another key to the garage?' Mr. Budd asked the bank manager.

'There's a spare in the key cabinet,' Mr. Fisk replied.

'Would you get it please, sir?' requested the superintendent. 'We need to ascertain if the Daimler is still there, and I'll be very surprised if it is.'

As Henry Apple approached the lift, the doors opened to reveal the police surgeon carrying his bag. 'Evening, Budd,' Melthorne greeted affably.

Mr. Budd guided the police surgeon to the vault, indicating the prone body on the floor. 'This is the bank's owner, Mr. Joshua Fisk. He's been shot twice.'

The vault was vacated while the police surgeon carried out a cursory examination. 'Shot quite recently,' he remarked. 'The body's still warm.'

Mr. Budd grunted. 'I urgently need to attend to a pressing matter, Melthorne.

I'll be back shortly.' He glanced at Brand. 'You see to things here while I take a look at this garage, will yer?'

'Certainly, sir,' answered the inspector.

Mr. Budd took from his waistcoat pocket one of his black cigars and looked at it with joyful anticipation. As he was searching for his box of matches, Henry Apple returned with the garage key.

'We'd better take a look,' Mr. Budd said to the bank manager and his sergeant.

A short while later, wreathed in evil-smelling cigar smoke, the three of them were staring into an empty garage.

'You're certain Mr. Fisk came in by car this mornin'?' Mr. Budd asked the bank manager.

'I didn't personally witness him arrive in his car,' admitted Mr. Apple. 'But Mr. Fisk always travelled to the bank in his Daimler, and I have no reason to believe he altered his routine.'

'Did he employ a chauffeur?'

'No. Mr. Fisk always drove himself.'

The big man blew out a lungful of smoke. 'It's a strong possibility that someone who knew him, or knew his habits, killed Mr. Fisk, locked him in the vault, stole the real money, and then pinched his car,' he explained to a bewildered Henry Apple. 'A large boot would be useful for transporting a great quantity of cash, don't you think? Do you have the registration?'

'It's JF10,' answered Henry Apple straightaway.

'Nice and easy to remember,' commented the big man with a meaningful glance at Leek. 'Put out an all-stations alert for this Daimler with a warning the driver is armed and dangerous.'

They walked back to the bank, the tip of Mr. Budd's cigar glowing in the dark as he drew upon it.

'Was Mr. Fisk married?' the detective asked the bank manager.

Henry Apple shook his head. 'No, he never married.'

They arrived at the staff entrance and went into the bank. Sergeant Leek went off to find a telephone while Mr. Budd gently pursued his line of questioning.

'Any brothers or sisters you might have

heard Mr. Fisk mention?'

Henry Apple paused by the lift doors, pursing his lips in recollection as he pushed the lift button. 'He never spoke of any,' he replied. 'Mr. Fisk kept himself to himself.'

'That doesn't surprise me,' murmured the big man. 'Do you know of anyone else who might have been here at the bank this evening after closing?'

'The staff usually left by six o'clock. The only person remaining when I left at six thirty was Mr. Fisk.'

The lift arrived. 'Down to the vault?' Mr. Apple checked, opening the lift gate.

'Yes, back to the vault. I'd better have a word with Doctor Melthorne, and I'm hopin' to get that cabinet open very soon,' said Mr. Budd, rubbing his chin. 'Now, I'm getting a picture of who Mr. Fisk is, but who's Fossett? You 'aven't mentioned 'im.'

Henry Apple gave a dry laugh as they entered the lift. 'Mr. Daniel Fossett died twenty years ago. His daughter inherited his share of the bank. She was an opera singer and went to America, having no interest in banking. Mr. Fisk bought her out, I believe.'

'The bank is totally owned by Joseph Fisk?'

'As far as I'm aware, yes,' answered the manager reluctantly, resenting Mr. Budd's right to pry into the bank's private affairs.

'What do you think will become of the bank?' continued Mr. Budd. 'Who do you think will inherit?'

Mr. Fisk closed the lift gate and pressed the 'Basement' button. 'I have no idea what Mr. Fisk's arrangements were,' he answered stiffly as they descended.

The area outside the vault was crowded. Doctor Melthorne had just completed his examination and was preparing to leave. He took Mr. Budd to one side.

'Shot twice through the heart at close range,' he informed him. 'Death would have been instantaneous, and as a result there was very little blood.'

'Time of death?' Mr. Budd requested.

'Very recent; this evening between eight and nine o'clock.'

'Not long before we arrived?'

'Exactly so,' confirmed the doctor.

Mr. Budd wasn't at all gratified to think that if he had arrived sooner, it might have been possible to save Fisk's life and arrest the Dutchman before he committed another murder. 'There was very little loss in body temperature,' Doctor Melthorne was saying as he finished packing his bag. 'You'll have my full report in the morning.' With a brief wave, he went towards the lift, which at that moment arrived with a police constable and a locksmith.

After a few minutes of working on the lock, the locksmith opened the doors of the steel cabinet. To Mr. Budd's disappointment, the cabinet was empty, but he expected no less. He was certain the Dutchman had cleared it out, taking with him all the real money and then stealing the Daimler to transport it. He began a systematic search of Joseph Fisk's office on the top floor but couldn't discover anything of immediate interest.

Before leaving the bank to visit Joseph Fisk's home in Chiswick, Mr. Budd had a brief discussion with Inspector Brand about interviewing the staff in the morning and making general enquiries of the neighbourhood in case anything unusual had been witnessed.

The superintendent was becoming increasingly worried about Glenda Lane. He knew she had no home telephone from working with her father. He put through a call to Wapping to see if anyone could call upon her in order to make certain she had arrived home safely, but no one from the night shift was available to make the visit. He thought of Constable Joe Bentley and obtained his telephone number. Bentley answered his telephone straightaway. Without going into detail, Mr. Budd asked if he would go to Stepney and check that Glenda was all right. Bentley was only too happy to oblige.

★   ★   ★

The house at Chiswick was a four-storey Georgian building overlooking the river, with its own mooring facility. The

214

banker's housekeeper, Mrs. Olive Samuels, eventually opened the door in her dressing gown. She was a tall powerful-looking woman with dark penetrating eyes, high cheekbones, and steel-grey hair in a bun, all of which enhanced her formidable expression. She possessed a natural air of authority that was unlike any housekeeper Mr. Budd had ever met, and not at all as he had imagined she would be.

'We're police officers,' he began, stifling a yawn. 'We're sorry to call at such a late hour.'

'What is it you want?' she demanded in a harsh voice. She was plainly irritated by the intrusion.

'You are Mrs. Olive Samuels?' Mr. Budd asked, showing her his warrant card.

'What's all this about?' she asked suspiciously. 'What right have you bothering people at this time of night?'

Mr. Budd patiently explained how Joseph Fisk had been found in the vault.

'Joseph's dead?' She stared at him in disbelief.

'I'm afraid there's no doubt about it,' answered the detective.

She fell back into the hall and slumped against the wall. 'How can this be?'

Mr. Budd briefly explained that the bank had been robbed, how Joseph Fisk had been murdered, and finally that his car had gone missing.

'This is terrible, terrible!' she reacted in horror, repeating the words over and over while gasping for breath. 'You're certain of this? There hasn't been a mistake?'

'There's no mistake, Mrs. Samuels,' Mr. Budd confirmed gently. 'Mr. Apple identified the body.'

'Mr. Apple?' she repeated, as if that made everything true. 'I can't believe this has happened to Joseph, just as things were improving. It's so unfair.'

'Life can be very unfair Mrs. Samuels,' murmured the stout man stoically.

'You think I don't know that?' she retorted, recovering a little of her former arrogance. 'I've suffered my fair share of unfairness, Superintendent. Who did this evil thing?'

'There's a man we're seeking to help

us in with our enquiries,' Mr. Budd answered cautiously.

It was clear the relationship between Mrs. Samuels and her employer was a close one and that his death had come as a great shock. While fighting hard to put on a brave face, she was near collapse.

'Would you like Sergeant Leek to brew a pot of tea, Mrs. Samuels? You might find it beneficial. You've had quite a shock.'

'I don't drink tea,' she snapped, staggering over to a sideboard. Grabbing a decanter, she poured out a generous measure of cognac into a crystal glass. She knocked the cognac back in one gulp and immediately replenished it. Clutching the glass tightly for comfort, she sat down on a large sofa, almost spilling the contents.

'Have you heard of a Dutchman who goes by the name of Peter Van der Horst?' Mr. Budd asked her.

'No, I haven't,' she answered immediately. 'Did he kill Joseph?'

'It's a possibility,' answered Mr. Budd vaguely.

'Why haven't you arrested him?' she demanded.

'We will arrest him when we find 'im.'

'You've lost him?'

'We're busy looking for 'im and don't expect 'im to get far.'

'Do you have any idea why Joseph has been — been — ' She couldn't bring herself to say it. 'Joseph was too kind. People took advantage of him.'

Mr. Budd had never known a bank manager who was taken advantage of, but he was pleased she'd provided him with the opening he was looking for.

'That's one reason why we came straight here, Mrs. Samuels, to find out why he was murdered. We'd like to take a look around Mr. Fisk's study.'

She looked as if she might refuse, but taking a deep breath gave a brief nod of assent, stood up shakily and, still clutching her glass of cognac, went over to the door.

They followed her out into the hall.

'I'll show you to his study,' she said, ascending the broad stairway. 'Please leave everything as you find it. Mr. Fisk wouldn't like his things disturbed.'

The banker's study was on the first floor. It was a tastefully furnished room with a regency walnut desk and a high-backed leather chair as its centrepiece. There were also a couple of easy chairs, occasional tables, two tall bookcases, a sideboard with decanters, and some interesting art on the walls. The overall effect was expensive without ostentation.

Mr. Budd studied several photographs displayed in expensive frames, focussing on one in particular that portrayed a family group outside a church that looked as if it might have been taken at a Christening. Another was a portrait of a woman.

'That's Joseph's mother,' Mrs. Samuels explained.

The telephone on the desk rang. They all stared at it as if answering it could only bring more bad news. Mrs. Samuels picked up the receiver and listened for a few moments.

'It's a Constable Bentley for you, Superintendent,' she said, handing Mr.

Budd the receiver.

Joe Bentley sounded concerned and agitated. He'd been over to Glenda's home in Stepney and rapped upon the door, but received no answer. The milk, delivered that morning, was still on the doorstep.

'She obviously never returned home,' he said.

'I feared that might be the case,' Mr. Budd agreed.

'Do you have any idea where she might be, sir?'

'I have no idea at all,' answered the detective truthfully.

'But surely you must think she's in some kind of danger, or you wouldn't have asked me to see if she was at home,' persisted Bentley. 'Is she in danger, sir?'

Mr. Budd paused, rubbing his chin contemplatively as he considered how best to deal with these questions. He couldn't be certain Glenda Lane was in any danger. He had no evidence to support that anything had happened to her at all. What if she had visited a friend and stayed the night? In that event, his concerns were totally without foundation. Though he possessed no definite evidence that she was in any danger, his common sense told him she might have ventured one step too far and got into serious trouble. He chose not to tell the constable that Glenda had gone to visit her father's room in Whitechapel, or that he'd taken her to the Monument. Nor did he disclose the murder of Mr. Fisk in Lombard Street. There seemed little point in making Bentley more anxious than he was already.

'I fear she may be in some difficulty. I have no supportive evidence to back that up other than intuition,' Mr. Budd admitted. 'I'd rather assume she needs help than ignore the signs. Let's hope she'll seek to communicate with us at her first opportunity.'

'I gave her my telephone number before she left Wapping to go home,' Bentley told him. 'In case she needed my assistance.'

'That's very useful,' said Mr. Budd. 'That was thoughtful of you, Constable Bentley. My best advice is to remain close to your instrument in the hope that she calls. If I get any further information regarding her whereabouts, I'll keep you informed. If she does call you, telephone the Yard at once. They'll know where to find me.' He replaced the receiver.

Mrs. Samuels, emboldened by the cognac, had obviously listened to every word of the detective's conversation with Bentley.

'Has something else happened?' she asked.

'I have reason to believe a woman has been abducted by the Dutchman, Peter Van der Horst,' he told her.

He watched her carefully through half-closed eyelids for a reaction, but there wasn't one. He began studying another photograph of a much younger Joseph Fisk at a coastal resort. Standing next to him was a man who possessed similar features but was a little taller, thinner, and maybe a few years older. He studied the photograph carefully before he turned the frame over. He was disappointed to see nothing written on the back of it.

'That's Joseph's brother Isaac,' Mrs. Samuels volunteered. 'He suffered terribly during the war. Being Jewish, he was sent to a concentration camp.'

'He lived in Germany before the war?' asked Mr. Budd with a glance at Sergeant Leek, who took out his notebook and began writing.

'Oh, yes.' She took a gulp of cognac, placing the glass on a small table before collapsing heavily into one of the easy chairs. 'He was living in Hamburg with Corinna.'

The big man raised an eyebrow. 'Corinna?'

'His wife,' she said, her eyebrows drawing together in a frown. 'I told Corinna many times that they should leave Germany, but she was in denial. Isaac was in denial too. They both were. When they eventually came to their senses and realised they had to leave, it was too late. They were arrested on the train on their way to the border, interrogated and sent to concentration camps.' Her eyes filled with tears which she irritably brushed away. 'That was the most dreadful part of it, being split up.

Isaac was sent to Sachsenhausen and poor Corinna to Mauthausen, where she died of starvation. It was terrible, very terrible and very sad.' Mrs. Samuels blew her nose.

'But Isaac survived?' Mr. Budd asked, holding his breath.

'Oh yes, Isaac survived, more by luck than management.' She fought down her anger. 'The SS wanted to murder them all,' she spat out, 'but the truck broke down.'

Mr. Budd was at a loss. 'The truck?'

Mrs. Samuels stared at him for a moment wistfully. 'Isaac Fisk was in the truck. On the third trip, the truck broke down.'

'Mrs. Samuels,' Mr. Budd addressed her kindly, 'I have no idea what you mean by the third trip and the truck breaking down. Please enlighten me.'

She sat up. 'I'd better start at the beginning. Now poor Joseph is dead, it won't matter so much.'

'What won't matter, Mrs. Samuels?' asked Mr. Budd, surveying her through half-closed eyes.

'Nothing matters!' she answered fiercely, clutching her fists until the knuckles went white. 'When Isaac arrived at Sachsenhausen, his talent was immediately evaluated with the usual German efficiency, and he was seconded to a segregated factory within the camp. He was forced to become part of a counterfeiting team working around the clock, engraving the plates the Germans required. The special team eventually produced one hundred and thirty-four million pounds' worth of fake English bank notes as part of Germany's plan to break the Bank of England. The German's called it Operation Bernard.' She looked up. 'You've heard of it?'

Mr. Budd nodded, and she continued.

'It was named after Major Bernard Krüger, the Nazi responsible for it. The counterfeiting team didn't remain in Sachsenhausen. They were transferred to another camp, Redl-Zipf, in Austria. At the beginning of May 1945, they were transferred again to the notorious Ebenezer camp, unaware the SS planned to murder them all. The Germans wanted to erase all trace of their activities.' She spoke slowly and intently. 'With only one truck available to transport all of them to Ebenezer, the transfer required three trips. Isaac Fisk was kept waiting until the third trip, and it was on that final journey that the truck broke down. They were force marched the rest of the journey to Ebenezer — a truly awful place. It was a place of such evil cruelty you couldn't imagine. The camp had a high death rate — nearly everyone died there. You see, Mr. Budd, the order from the higher echelons of the SS was for the counter-feiters to be liquidated together, and it was the delayed arrival of those in the third truck that saved all of them, thanks to the Germans' love of paperwork and obeying orders to the letter.' She squeezed her eyes shut, trying not to relive some awful horror.

'How were they saved, Mrs. Samuels?' asked Mr. Budd quietly.

She opened her eyes and looked up, startled. 'Yes, they were saved on 6th May 1945. The camp was liberated by the Americans.'

'You seem very well informed,' murmured Mr. Budd.

'I ought to be. I'm Corinna's sister.'

'Ah, that explains it.'

'I married my husband Greg over here before the war — Greg Samuels. He was killed in the Blitz. Our house was destroyed and I had nowhere to go. Joseph was very kind to me and offered me a place here. To stop any gossip about a man and a woman living in a house together unmarried, we thought it would make things easier if I became the housekeeper.'

'I understand,' said Mr. Budd.

She shrugged. 'Which after all is what I am — I've looked after this house since the war.'

The big man nodded. 'Isaac Fisk was your brother-in-law. Did he visit often?'

Mrs. Samuels looked up at the ceiling as she recollected. 'A year ago he came over from Holland for a couple of weeks.'

'Where does he live in Holland, Mrs. Samuels?' He was watching her very closely in his sleepy way and thought he detected a momentary hesitation before she replied.

'Isaac was always an artist, a very talented one,' she said, getting up and walking over to the window. She looked out at the river. The Thames was in darkness except for reflected lights from the riverbank that danced like spirits upon the water. She drew the curtains and turned into the room.

'He was born here in England and in 1935 married my sister, a fellow artist. They went to live in Hamburg, where Corinna taught art at the university while Isaac etched portraits for a living onto copper plate. They were very happy together until war broke out. Isaac lives in Amsterdam in Van der Hoopstraat with my brother. We're German Jews. Our surname is Schuster and we're originally from Danzig.'

'Were you aware of any irregularities with Mr. Fisk's bank recently?' Mr. Budd asked her.

'There were some financial problems a while ago, and we — Joseph, was quite concerned for the bank's future,' she answered reluctantly. 'A few months ago he told me things had improved. I don't know much about banking, Superintendent.'

Mr. Budd hesitated, then choosing his words carefully, he asked, 'Do you have any reason to think that after the war, Isaac Fisk might have continued to practise the counterfeiting operation he learned while in Sachsenhausen?'

A flicker of fear passed across her eyes. 'I would hope not, Superintendent,' she said with a sigh of exasperation. 'Why don't you ask him?' She picked up her glass and left the room.

Mr. Budd was sorry to have annoyed her, but was relieved she'd gone. Her departure gave him the opportunity to search Joseph Fisk's desk without scrutiny. In a drawer he found a bound sheaf of papers representing the bank's provisional accounts to April of the previous year.

He flicked through the pages until he came to the profit and loss figures. The numbers showed the bank was losing a considerable amount of money. He moved on to the balance sheet and paused, scratching his chin. The accounts made it quite clear that Fisk and Fossett were insolvent. He found some loose progress sheets outlining recent profit and loss figures and could see at a glance they showed a healthy improvement in the bank's performance, with profits moving into positive territory from last August.

He allowed himself a small smile of triumph, because the figures made it clear to him that almost miraculously in the short space of five months, the bank's fortunes had reversed. He knew that miracles seldom happened on this scale in the current financial climate. The bank's sudden success was likely due to exchanging a large number of counterfeit banknotes for real ones, which had then been paid into the bank as the fake proceeds from fictitious contracts.

'That's what I was hoping to find,' he said to Leek as he folded the sheets up and tucked them into an inside pocket of his coat. 'I think we can leave now.'

'It's been a difficult day,' Sergeant Leek commented. 'I'm ready for me bed.'

The telephone on the desk rang again. He reached out to it, but Mrs. Samuels had already lifted the receiver downstairs and called up.

'Superintendent, it's Constable Bentley again.'

9

Feeling more like an unlawful intruder than a policewoman, Glenda Lane approached the scullery door of the house. Her childhood memories were slowly returning, and she hoped she would find what she was seeking. She reached out a hand to the back of a water butt and groped with her fingers for a key she remembered was once kept there. Her fingers touched something slimy which felt like a slug or a snail, and then a wet metallic object. Much to her astonishment, after all the intervening years, a key was still there, forgotten until now and pitted with grime.

Stepping back and looking up at the windows, she made certain there were no lights on in the house. With numb fingers, she inserted the key in the back-door lock. It turned easily. Luckily the door hadn't been bolted on the inside, and she was able to lift the latch and push the door inwards, pausing when the hinges made a protesting squeak. But she had created enough of a gap to squeeze through.

The kitchen felt wonderfully warm after being out in the cold. She crossed to the stove and pulled the front down, and a warm glow flooded out into the room. She enjoyed the warmth for a few moments, allowing it to thaw her out while her eyes fastened on the prone body of the swarthy man on the floor, the man she'd heard called Isaac. His sightless eyes, reflecting the red glow from the stove, stared at the kitchen ceiling and, like the mannequin, made her feel uneasy.

She forced herself to kneel down in order to search through the dead man's pockets, trying to avoid his eyes. All she found was a key that looked as if it fitted a mortice lock. She slipped the key into her pocket and stood up.

On the kitchen table was a storm lantern, but it was too big for what she wanted. A candle would do better, and she found a box in the pantry. She chose a slim one that wouldn't give out too much light and lit it from the hot coals of the stove. Holding the candle in one hand, she ventured out into the hallway, the candle light invading the dark sufficiently for her to see where she was going.

Carefully, she made her way up the staircase and succeeded in reaching the landing without making a sound. She paused, listening. From the front bedroom came a nasal cacophony that resembled a discordant orchestra of the devil tuning up, long whistling sounds reaching a crescendo before tumbling into deep grunts, wheezing, and long snorts, only to rise in pitch once more. It was heaven to her ears, because his snoring signified the Dutchman was in a deep sleep. All the while the noise continued, he would be oblivious to her presence.

Slowly she turned the handle and cracked open the door, shielding the candle flame with her other hand. She peered into the bedroom that she had once slept in as a child. In the soft flickering light of the candle, she saw the

Dutchman stretched out on a crude metal bed in a whisky-induced stupor. He was fully clothed, still wearing his shoes, lying on his back with a blanket pulled half over him. His mouth was open, and it was from this orifice of broken teeth that the hellish noises blasted forth.

On a bedside table in front of her, the keys of the Daimler rested next to an automatic pistol. She opened the door further and slipped across the threshold into the room. She held her breath, never for a moment taking her eyes off the figure on the bed. Holding the candle aloft, taking one cautious step at a time, she moved up to the table. On the third step, a loose board gave a protesting creak with a noise that sounded to her ears like a pistol shot.

She froze, staring at the Dutchman's mouth, which had snapped shut. With a long indrawn rasping groan of protest, it opened again. The huge body heaved itself onto its side, facing away from her. Her heart pounding, she slowly breathed in, filling her lungs, and then slowly breathed out with a sigh of relief. One more step and she was able to lean forward with an outstretched arm to grip the automatic and lift it off the table top. She felt its weight and deadly assurance, and permitted herself a quick smile of satisfaction.

With the automatic in one hand and the candle in the other, she had no free hand, so she spilt a little molten wax on the table top and stuck the candle in it. The Daimler keys made a small metallic sound as she gathered them up and slipped them into the pocket of her coat.

She took a set of handcuffs out of her shoulder bag and, leaning towards the sleeping body, fastened one half around the bedframe. Now came the tricky bit. The wrist of the Dutchman's right hand was exposed. Holding her breath again, she gently snapped the other half of the cuff around his wrist and nimbly leapt back, retracing to the door. She slipped off the safety catch, raised the automatic, and switched on the light.

The Dutchman was in such a deep sleep he didn't react at all.

She moved around to the foot of the

bed and gave the metal frame a vicious kick. 'Wake up!' she shouted.

The snoring stopped abruptly. Grunting, the Dutchman turned over, rucking up the blanket beneath him.

She kicked the bed again. 'You need to wake up!' she repeated.

The Dutchman groaned and produced several explosive sounds.

'Wake up! Come on, wake up!'

A bleary eye opened and then closed.

She kicked the bed for the third time.

The eye opened again and the Dutchman rolled over with a snort. It was clear to her he didn't know where he was or what was happening.

She poked his leg viciously with the barrel of the automatic.

Opening both red and bleary eyes, he tried to focus on the gun in her hand. As he finally realised what was happening, his face contorted into a mask of rage. 'What the hell?'

'You're under arrest,' she informed him in as strong a voice as she could muster.

'Who are you?' he asked, slurring his words. 'The hell I . . . '

The Dutchman started to swing off the bed and was about to raise his fist when he was jerked back and realised he was cuffed to the bedframe. He stared at her malevolently.

'Stay still or I'll shoot!' she threatened nervously. 'Don't think I don't mean it. I was trained to shoot during the war. I shan't miss.'

There was something menacing in the tone of her voice that convinced the Dutchman she meant what she said. He reluctantly fell back onto the bed, glaring at her with contempt.

'I've seen yer before,' he said thickly.

'I'm WPC Glenda Lane of Thames Division,' she said proudly in a confident voice, now that she had the upper hand.

'Lane?' He looked at her groggily. 'Yer name is Lane?'

His emphasis on her surname prompted her to explain further, like casting a fly as a lure in the expectation of a bite. 'Detective Inspector Derek Lane was my father!'

The man with the scar frowned, and then threw his head back and laughed contemptuously. 'Did he put you up to this — sending a woman to do a man's job?'

'Did you know my father?'

The Dutchman evaded the question. 'How did you find me? How did you get here?'

'You drove me here,' she told him, pleased at the look of surprise on his face.

'I drove you?' he asked in disbelief.

'I was in the back of the car you stole.'

His eyes narrowed. 'You were at the bank?'

'I watched you load up the money. Why did you bring it here to my old home?'

The Dutchman sneered. 'You better ask your father that question.'

'That won't be possible. My father was pulled out of the Thames early this morning. He died doing his duty.'

The Dutchman laughed. 'Doing his duty? That's funny! You're going to get into a lot of trouble,' he warned her. 'You don't know what a mistake you're making.'

'I'm calling the police,' she told him, lowering the gun, satisfied he was properly secured to the bed rail.

The Dutchman laughed drunkenly and didn't seem bothered. 'That's funny! I thought you *were* the police?'

'You can explain everything to them,' she said, ignoring his jibe.

'I explain nothing,' he spat defiantly, holding her stare with glittering eyes. 'There's no telephone here.'

'I'll manage,' she retorted brusquely. 'Who was that man you murdered in the kitchen?'

'Find out!' he snarled.

Before she left, she hurriedly searched the property. When she came to the cellar door, she found it locked, fitted with a new mortice. As she felt in her pocket for the key she'd taken from the dead man in the kitchen, she also found the crumpled piece of paper Joe Bentley had given her with his telephone number written on it. She felt comfort in the knowledge she had it and carefully stowed it away.

Inserting the key in the lock, she gave it a turn. The door opened inwards, revealing a flight of steep stone steps leading down. She switched on the cellar light and an amazing sight met her eyes.

The cellar in which apples had once been stored had been transformed into a counterfeiting workshop. The centrepiece was a complex flatbed printing press. Next to the press was a guillotine on a steel stand. Stacked beside the guillotine on a separate table were freshly printed five-pound notes, four to a sheet, waiting to be trimmed. Against the far wall was a bench with a microscope, magnifying lenses, racks of engraver's tools, and shelves with bottles of liquids. In a corner were cans of printing ink. At the foot of the cellar steps was a pile of bags and boxes she assumed were the ones unloaded from the boot of the Daimler.

She hurried down the steps and opened the top boxes. They contained hundreds of thousands of pounds' worth of cash, in packets wrapped and stamped by the Bank of England.

She was filled with excitement at her discovery and what she'd be able to report. Returning to the kitchen, she lit the storm lantern with a spill from the stove. As the wick caught and the flame grew, she caught sight of a splash of red paint on the base that triggered some long-lost memory. How were her father and her old home connected with the counterfeiters?

She hurried out to the barn and slipped inside. Illuminated by the lantern she carried, she recognised it as a place where she'd often played as a child when the back wall had been stacked with bales of hay. Holding the lantern aloft, she lifted the boot lid of the Daimler and peered inside. It was empty apart from a blanket. She put down the lantern while she opened the driver's door and climbed in, started the engine and switched on the headlights. She extinguished the lantern and placed it on a bench.

Her priority was to find a telephone box. She drove the big car out of the barn, past the house, and along the track, which became Turnpike Lane. She knew that the nearest village was Marshford, and that she'd find a telephone box there. She turned right onto the Colchester road and further on she came to a fork, remembering to keep to the left. The sky was totally overcast and she could see no sign of the sea, which she knew must be somewhere ahead. It was a relief to know she wasn't lost when eventually the headlights picked up a signpost confirming Marshford was a mile further along the road.

Her mind was in turmoil as she drove the big car. She knew her father had rented the property when they came down from the midlands shortly after she was born, and when they left to live in London the landlord would have rented it out to someone else. Now, all these years later, it was the headquarters of the counterfeiting operation. That her father could be involved in such an operation was too horrible to contemplate. Her mind went back to the original problem she had wrestled with — what had her father been doing with a shop window dummy stuffed full of counterfeit cash on the river in the dark hours before dawn?

As she drove into the village of Marshford, the headlights illuminated fleetingly the village school she had once attended and the comer shop where she had bought sweets. All was in darkness except for a solitary illuminated telephone box on the green. She pulled up outside it.

What should she do now? She wasn't officially on police business. She could get into considerable trouble for taking matters into her own hands.

Retrieving the scrap of paper Joe Bentley had given her, she decided to telephone him.

★ ★ ★

Bentley had returned from Stepney a very worried man. He had resolved to stay up all night if necessary in case Glenda telephoned. He was on his third cup of camp coffee, having emptied the bottle, when the bell began ringing. Picking up the receiver, his heart missed a beat as he recognised Glenda's voice. She sounded very much in control.

'Joe, I'm sorry if I've woken you. Are you properly awake?'

'I haven't been asleep. What's happened, Glenda?' he asked, desperate for information.

'I've got quite a lot to tell you and some things I'd like you to do, if you wouldn't mind.'

'Where are you? Is everything all right?'

'You'll need a notebook,' she said firmly.

He'd already put one open by the telephone. 'I've got one here.' Questions were tumbling into his mind so fast he could hardly get them out. 'Where are you? What's happened?'

'Calm down, Joe. I'm trying to explain. First you need to know that I'm calling you from a call box in Marshford village. I haven't much change. If anything goes wrong, call me back on this number.'

She read out the number of the call box. He scribbled it down and repeated it. 'Marshford? Where's Marshford?'

'It's in Essex, about four miles from Shinglesea and about three miles from East Shorewell,' she answered crisply.

Bentley couldn't hide his horror at how

far away she was. 'You're up near the Colne estuary? What the blazes are you doing there, Glenda?'

She could hardly contain her excitement. 'Listen carefully. I've just witnessed a murder and arrested the man responsible.'

'You've done *what!*' Joe nearly dropped his pencil. 'Crikey, Glenda!'

'Joe — it was the Dutchman!'

'You've arrested the Dutchman? How did you manage that?'

'I've handcuffed him to a bed.'

'Whereabouts?' Bentley asked, bewildered.

She didn't want to tell him he was in the bedroom of her childhood home because she hadn't been able to reconcile that fact herself. 'I've discovered the headquarters of the counterfeiting operation. Please write that down.'

'I'm writing everything down.' He scribbled notes in a daze; he couldn't believe what he was hearing. Suddenly he stopped writing and a big grin spread across his face as a thought occurred to him. 'You're not having me on, are you?

Have you been to a party? Are you feeling tipsy?'

Glenda couldn't stop herself getting angry. 'You need to take this seriously, Joe. This is not a joke. Please, try to be sensible. This is really urgent!'

By the tone of her voice he realized he'd made a silly mistake, and felt a fool. 'I'm sorry. It's just that it all sounds so implausible.'

'I know where hundreds of thousands of pounds in cash have been taken, stolen from Fisk and Fossett — that's a bank in Lombard Street. You'll need to inform Superintendent Budd at Scotland Yard as soon as we've finished talking, and tell him everything I'm telling you.'

'I've spoken to him already tonight. He asked me to go round to your house to make sure you were all right. When I told him you weren't at home, he was very worried about you.'

'Has he been to the bank?'

'He didn't say. You'd better give me the address where the Dutchman is before you forget.'

'Oh yes, the address — it's Well End in Turnpike Lane.'

Bentley repeated the address as he wrote it down. 'I've got that.'

'Good. Now, I need you to contact the police at Shorewell. Ask them to come at once to meet me at this telephone box in Marshford village — they can't miss it. I shall be waiting in a large black Daimler to take them to where all this has happened, about a mile and a half from here. The moment I hang up, you need to hurry and make those calls. It's perishing cold up here, but I'll keep the car window cracked open so I can hear the bell ringing. I want you to call me back when you've made the calls.'

'I'll contact the superintendent and Shorewell right away,' Bentley promised. 'Please be careful, Glenda.'

'Don't worry,' she assured him. 'I can protect myself.'

'These are dangerous people.'

'I've got an automatic pistol.'

Bentley nearly dropped the receiver. 'Good heavens, Glenda! An automatic! You won't attempt to use it, will you?'

'I'll use it if I have to,' she said firmly.

'You have no authority to use it,' he warned, and immediately regretted saying it.

'I'll be all right, Joe,' Glenda answered calmly. 'I was trained to shoot during the war. You won't forget to — ' She broke off, blinded as powerful headlights lit up the call box. A big car was heading straight towards her.

'Sorry — headlights are blinding me. Someone's turned up.'

'What's that?' Bentley was shouting into the mouthpiece, trying to visualise what was going on, but feeling completely helpless. He could hear some commotion, and then a male voice was speaking outside the call box, but it was distorted. He couldn't make out what was being said.

'Glenda, what's happening?'

There was a scrabbling sound as she grabbed the receiver.

'Hang on a minute!' She was shouting, sounding confused.

He knew she was in some kind of trouble. Why had a car drawn up at a telephone box in a remote village at that late hour?

'Glenda!'

There was no answer.

'Glenda!' he repeated frantically.

He gripped the receiver tightly and stared at it. His head was in a whirl as his imagination conjured up endless variations of her plight.

'Glenda! Can you hear me? What's happening?'

There was a click. The line went dead.

10

Bentley reported to Mr. Budd everything Glenda Lane had told him before they were cut off. As he replaced the receiver, the big superintendent's brain was in turmoil.

'I've been a fool,' he admitted to Leek, who visibly brightened at his superior's confession.

'You don't admit to it very often,' said his sergeant.

'We've been led up the garden path.'

'Please don't remind me of that,' said Leek, reverting to his melancholy self.

'I've been racking my brains to work out how they smuggled the notes in dummies that were checked by customs, and the answer was simple — they didn't! The dummies, the studio, the house in Paradise Street and, I believe, Detective Inspector Lane rowing that boat with the dummy stuffed with cash, were all an elaborate diversion to send us on a wild goose chase. All of it was a subterfuge to divert us from discovering the truth.' He paused. 'We have to get to that address in Essex. Constable Bentley has suggested a quick way of getting us there.'

The stout detective was now in no doubt Glenda Lane was in serious danger. He arranged for Scotland Yard to contact Shorewell police and authorise them to dispatch a car immediately to the address Glenda had provided. He personally spoke to Detective Inspector Morrison at Shorewell police station and asked him to keep a look out for Glenda, providing him with a description of her. He also instructed Morrison to go through the village of Marshford and keep a lookout for a black Daimler. He was certain they would find the vehicle abandoned.

Bentley had persuaded him the quickest way to get to the address Glenda had provided was to go by water. After seeking authorisation from Superintendent Ramsay that he could commandeer the *Black Rose* and crew it with Constable Bentley and Sergeant Reeves,

Mr. Budd made an additional request for Shorewell police to meet them at West Shorewell Pier.

'You wanted to see the river, didn't you?' he asked Sergeant Leek. 'Well, now's yer opportunity.'

'I can't see anything in the dark,' moaned Leek, looking miserable as thoughts of going home to his bed receded.

A short while later, Bentley and Reeves picked them up from Joshua Fisk's private mooring, and Mr. Budd found himself cautiously climbing aboard the Dutchman's sleek and powerful launch, followed by an equally apprehensive Leek.

Bentley introduced them to Sergeant Reeves. 'I hope I've been reliably informed,' Mr. Budd confided to Reeves, giving Bentley a penetrating stare, 'that this boat is the fastest way to get to Shorewell Island.'

Sergeant Reaves returned a grin which Mr. Budd found disconcerting. 'This launch is the fastest way to get anywhere,' he confirmed. 'It should get us to the

Colne Estuary by first light, sir.'

'Let's not waste any more time then,' Mr. Budd advised, rubbing his hands to warm them up. 'Where do we sit?'

'Those two comfortable seats at the back would probably suit you best, sir,' suggested Reeves. 'There's sturdy handles on either side.'

'What are the handles for?' asked Leek innocently.

'To hold on to,' said Bentley. 'We'll be going fast, and the sea gets choppy when we get out into the estuary. If you take your hats off, you'd best put these on.' He produced a couple of sou'westers to protect their heads and oilskin jackets to put over their coats.

'Can you see where you're going in this fog?' Mr. Budd asked warily as he struggled into his jacket and then climbed onto the leather seat.

'This fog will clear once we get out of London. It should be a clear night and not too windy,' predicted Bentley cheerfully, turning the ignition key.

The high-performance Cadillac Eldorado V8 engines, each capable of producing 325hp, growled into life. Sergeant Reeves was already slackening off the forward rope. 'All clear,' he shouted.

Bentley switched on the navigation lights, and two powerful spotlights mounted forward of the windscreen. A wide stretch of the river sprang out of the darkness as they swung away from the small mooring and steered out into midstream. Bentley pulled back on the throttle. The two engines responded like hounds let off the leash.

Mr. Budd felt himself pushed back into his seat. Beneath him began a deep throbbing that promised plenty more power was available when needed. As the screws bit the water, the powerful launch surged forward. In next to no time, they had passed under Tower Bridge and were leaving the London docklands behind them, heading for Tilbury, turbulent water spreading out behind them as a huge wake.

With Tilbury behind them and the shore receding, Bentley pulled the throttle back further and unleashed the full power of the engines. The *Black Rose* responded magnificently, flying over the waves and smacking down hard onto the water, the twin screws pushing it over 60mph. The red lights of marker buoys guided them as they headed towards the English Channel, the shore line invisible except when marked by the occasional twinkling light. As the estuary widened, and a crosswind produced choppy waves, the prow of the launch sliced through them. Having cleared one wave, they crashed immediately into another, the hull bucking as they were propelled relentlessly onward, sending up huge bursts of ice-cold water from the prow that exploded onto the windscreen and sloughed off as a drenching salty spray.

Mr. Budd realised the full necessity of the handles as he held on for grim death to prevent being flung out of his seat. His face streamed with spray as his bones jostled and shook every time the launch smacked down onto water, which to the stout superintendent's buttocks felt like concrete. When the boat struck a particularly high wave, both he and his sergeant were lifted off their seats, only to be slammed down hard again. Mr. Budd was sure his spine was being slowly compressed with each wave trough and became convinced he must be now at least a foot shorter than when he'd come on board.

'Fabulous isn't she, sir?' Bentley shouted enthusiastically above the noise.

'Exhilarating,' grunted Mr. Budd with heavy sarcasm.

He wondered how he'd ever allowed Bentley to persuade him that travelling by boat was a sensible plan. The thought of a ride in the back of a warm and comfortable police Wolseley felt very desirable at that moment, but very unattainable. He forced all thoughts of comfort out of his mind while he seriously considered what death by drowning might really be like.

Bentley slowed down for a few minutes to allow Sergeant Reeves to produce cups of hot coffee for everyone from a thermos and a nip of brandy from a flask, for which they were all grateful.

'Bit of an adventure, eh, Leek?' shouted

Mr. Budd with bravado in his sergeant's ear.

'I didn't think it would be like this,' Leek moaned, clutching his stomach. 'Me insides feel queer.'

'What's that?' asked Mr. Budd as Leek's words were ripped away by the wind and the hull slapping the waves.

'Me insides feel queer,' Leek repeated louder.

The superintendent smiled. 'You probably need a hearty breakfast,' he suggested.

Leek looked at Mr. Budd with a sour expression. 'I couldn't eat anythin',' he said. 'I'd be sick as a dog.'

* * *

As Glenda stepped out of the call box, the car headlights were blinding her, and she put up a hand to shield her eyes. She heard a car door open, followed by the sound of feet crunching on gravel. She'd first thought the car drawn up at the kerb might be a police car, but as a figure came into view, she realised it wasn't and struggled for a moment to put a name to the face of the man approaching.

'Mr. Frobisher?' she said in surprise, remembering him from his visit to Wapping that morning. 'You're a long way from the Bank of England.'

She felt threatened by his sudden and unexpected appearance in such a lonely place, because she couldn't think of a rational explanation to explain why he was there. All her senses were alert telling her there was something seriously amiss with the situation. She decided to play along as if nothing was untoward.

Frobisher, who had recognised the Daimler as belonging to Joseph Fisk, was staring at it with a frown on his face, wondering how it had got there. He turned to Glenda, scrutinising her closely. 'I know you, don't I?'

'I'm WPC Lane,' she answered crisply. 'I met you this morning, sir — Thames Division at Wapping.'

Frobisher nodded his head, his frown deepening. 'That's quite right. I didn't recognise you out of uniform. Of course, you're Derek's daughter.'

She didn't like the familiarity with

which he used her father's Christian name, though she knew there was a rational explanation.

'You first worked with my father during the war, didn't you, sir?'

He nodded. 'You remember?'

'Yes, I remember,' she said. 'It was during the time he worked for the Intelligence Service.'

Her heart started pounding as she tried to fathom why she was having a conversation with Frobisher in the middle of the night at this remote location in Essex. The only explanation she could come up with was that he was in the counterfeiting operation up to his neck. He must know all about her old house, otherwise why would he be on this particular road? She had to play for time — surely the police must be on their way. Her hand slipped into her coat pocket and her fingers searched to get a grip on the automatic. She slipped off the safety catch.

'We were investigating German counterfeit operations,' Frobisher was saying. 'Your father was a smart man.'

'But not smart enough for you?' she retorted angrily.

All trace of the city gentleman immediately vanished. 'He was too smart for his own good,' Frobisher told her, his voice callous and hard-edged.

'Is that why he ended up in the river?'

'You should have left well alone instead of poking your nose into business that didn't concern you,' he answered with a cold stare. 'What are you doing up here with Fisk's Daimler?'

'It was stolen,' she told him. 'I'm returning it. It's what the police do.'

She could shoot Frobisher and this confrontation would be over. But where would that leave her? Judge, jury, and executioner, and a serious enquiry into her conduct.

Frobisher produced his own revolver.

If she fired now from inside her pocket, she might miss. From his superior position, Frobisher was unlikely to. All she would achieve by firing would be to accelerate her own death. She braced herself for the shock of a bullet. Would he shoot her and leave her for dead? By the look on his face, he was considering that option; but, changing his mind, he kept the gun aimed at her while he rummaged for a length of rope in his car boot. He found a short length of sash.

'It occurs to me you might be of more use alive. Put your hands behind your back. Don't try anything or you'll force me to shoot you.'

As he tied her wrists together securely, she realised her life had been temporarily spared because he preferred to keep her as a hostage.

'That's better,' he said with satisfaction when he'd finished. 'Who were you calling when I arrived?'

'The police. They're on their way.'

'Then we'd better not waste any more time,' he said, taking her arm in a strong grip and forcing her around to the passenger side, where he pushed her roughly into the car.

He went over to the Daimler, opened the boot, and gave a grunt of satisfaction when he found it empty. He returned to his own car and got behind the wheel, gunning the engine into life. He put his foot down and they sped away from the scene, leaving the Daimler abandoned outside the call box.

Glenda sat uncomfortably in the passenger seat, hunched forward, her arms behind her back. The Dutchman's automatic was still in her pocket, though she couldn't reach it. She now regretted not having used it while she had the chance. With the knowledge she now possessed, how could this man ever let her go?

Frobisher was obviously on his way to Well End, though he hadn't confirmed it. He was no doubt anxious to get his share of the cash the Dutchman had stolen from the bank. How would he react when he discovered the Dutchman handcuffed to a bed? More to the point, how would the Dutchman behave towards her if Frobisher released him? She tried to shut out the voice in her head that told her she hadn't long to live, whatever the outcome. She'd be killed and her body dumped somewhere it wouldn't be found. She thought of Joe . . . poor Joe would be upset.

On the positive side, Mr. Budd must have been alerted by now, and the Shorewell police as well. Maybe the police were at Well End already, and Frobisher was driving into a trap. That thought made her feel better. Her situation wasn't all hopeless; there was a good chance she would be rescued. She still didn't know why they had chosen Well End to be their headquarters, however; and who were they? Were the Dutchman and Frobisher part of the same gang? Was Frobisher the boss? How did her father fit into the picture? Who was the dead man, Isaac? There were endless questions to be answered.

'Why are you visiting my old house?' she asked.

'Your father told me about it during the war when we were working together. You'd just moved to Stepney. We started this in Amsterdam, but we soon realised it was impractical. Smuggling large amounts of fake cash into England was an unnecessary complication that invited discovery. I needed a base of operations in this country far away from prying eyes.

That was when I remembered Well End. I contacted the owner and made an offer he couldn't refuse. I bought the place about a year ago.'

The irony of the situation didn't escape her. 'While my father was investigating your counterfeit operation, the banknotes were being printed in the cellar of our old home?'

'You've poked your nose into the cellar, have you?'

'After I arrested the Dutchman,' she said, interested to see what effect that information would have.

Frobisher laughed. 'You arrested Van der Horst? How did you manage that?'

'I handcuffed him to the bedframe while he was sleeping. He drank a bottle of whisky and shot a man called Isaac.'

Frobisher stiffened, and she could see he hadn't been expecting that piece of news. 'He shot him in cold blood,' she added for greater effect. 'His body is in the kitchen.'

Frobisher sighed. 'Some men are natural killers, and he's one of them.'

'The Dutchman is this man Van der Horst?'

'Peter Van der Horst is a ruthless man who attracts too much attention. I first met him in Amsterdam through Isaac — forged passports, that kind of thing. We needed a strong man to clean up after us and Van der Horst was already on the spot feeding work from the criminal underworld to Isaac. He got rid of a German, Dieter Kretschmann — the man who supplied us with the paper. Men who can be trusted to carry out that kind of clean-up operation are very hard to find.'

'You mean criminals who commit murder?' she said bitterly. 'The Dutchman wants all the money for himself, doesn't he? He must be a big threat to you.' She was thinking that if Frobisher and the Dutchman killed one another, justice would be served and she would be out of danger, but it was an unlikely scenario. 'Did you come up here to kill him?' she asked.

'I have a clean exit except for two major problems.'

'What are they?'

'Van der Horst and you,' he answered bluntly as they reached the end of Turnpike Lane and the car headlights picked out the entrance gate to Well End.

★　★　★

Looking out to sea, the group aboard the *Black Rose* could discern a pale ribbon of light on the horizon — the faint cold grey of early dawn. Along the coast, twinkling lights were springing up as they navigated the Colne Estuary heading towards Shinglesea Creek.

The water was high as they approached Shinglesea Landing stage, which gave it the appearance of being further out from the shoreline than it actually was.

'High tide,' Bentley pointed out to Mr. Budd as Sergeant Reeves prepared to tie up. He waved his hand towards the shore. 'At low tide this is all mud.'

Mr. Budd eyed the water surrounding him with consternation as he removed his dripping jacket and sou'wester and returned them to Bentley. He picked up his wet hat and, shaking drops of water out of it, placed it on his head. The boat was bobbing slightly on the swell as he did his best to climb from the launch to the landing stage with dignity, feeling wobbly and clutching onto a guardrail for support.

He stood for a few moments to get his breath back and savoured the feeling of being on terra firma. He looked out to sea to the brightening horizon, thinking how good it was to be alive and vowing never to travel by speedboat again as long as he lived. He lighted a black cigar and inhaled the acrid smoke deeply, savouring the moment. Then he followed Sergeant Leek and Joe Bentley along the narrow wooden bridge of slatted timbers and wooden posts with the waves almost lapping at their feet. The bridge crossed the water to the shore where a short path took them up to the road. A detective constable from the local police was parked up, waiting to take them to Well End. Sergeant Reeves remained with the boat.

As the local constable drove them through Marshford, they saw the telephone box Glenda had used to call

Bentley. The Daimler was still parked by the kerb.

There was no sign of anyone.

★   ★   ★

Frobisher turned his car around in front of the barn and parked up. He switched off the headlights, slipped the ignition keys into his pocket, and got out. He opened the passenger door and said to Glenda, 'Get out of the car.'

Glenda swung her legs out and tried to stand up, but lost her balance. Frobisher grabbed her arm and yanked her out. He swung her roughly up against the side of the vehicle and searched her pockets. He found her handcuff key in one pocket and discovered the automatic in another. He balanced the heavy weapon in his hand. 'What's this?'

'I took it from the Dutchman,' she answered.

He looked at her with a new respect. 'Van der Horst is getting careless.' He smirked, putting the automatic in his coat pocket. 'Not just careless, but rather stupid. Let's go and see how Peter's feeling.'

Holding Glenda firmly by her arm, Frobisher let them in through the front door and turned on the hall light. Looking through into the kitchen, he immediately saw the body of Isaac sprawled on the floor but didn't say anything or pay the body further attention. He marched her up the stairs in front of him, pressing his gun into her back.

With no means of saving herself if she stumbled, Glenda was careful to keep her balance as she ascended the stairs. When she reached the landing, she could see that the bedroom door was open and the room was in darkness.

Frobisher pushed her roughly to one side, entered the bedroom and turned on the light. He saw at once that the room was empty. The handcuffs dangled from the bedframe, but the Dutchman was no longer attached to them.

Glenda noticed that the candle she had left burning on the bedside table had gutted in a pool of wax that had run off dripping onto the floor. Beside the remains of the candle was a handcuff key. She asked herself where the Dutchman had got the key from, and then remembered what had happened to Superintendent Budd and Sergeant Leek at the house in Paradise Street, and realised he must have acquired the key there. He'd had the means to escape the cuffs all the time.

She was annoyed with herself for not checking thoroughly, but wisely hadn't wanted to get too close to the Dutchman. She wasn't sure with whom she felt most vulnerable, the Dutchman or Frobisher. How could she manage to contend with both of them with her hands tied behind her back? That she was in a bit of a pickle was an understatement; neither would let her go willingly.

Frobisher looked unnerved at the sight of the dangling handcuffs. Where was the Dutchman? He quickly checked the rooms at the top of the house and returned to the landing. There was neither sight nor sound of him.

Glenda indicated the dangling hand-cuffs by jerking her head. 'Can you use them and handcuff me with my hands at the front?' she pleaded. 'Otherwise I'll slow you down. I can't keep my balance like this.'

Frobisher was about to refuse, but seeing how the rope was chaffing the skin of her wrists, changed his mind. He grabbed the key off the bedside table and, leaning across the bed, retrieved the handcuffs. 'I'm going to untie you. Don't try anything,' he warned, loosening the bonds.

Once free, she massaged her wrists before putting on the cuffs. He checked they were securely fastened and pushed her onto the landing. 'Go down first,' he instructed.

'You don't trust him, do you?'

'I don't trust anyone,' he snapped.

Glenda assumed the Dutchman had to be somewhere close and felt a shiver of fear run up her spine. She descended the stairs to the hall below, with Frobisher close behind her. They were both listening acutely for any tell-tale sound that would indicate the Dutchman was still in the house. He'd had plenty of time to escape on foot, but if the money was still in the cellar, she didn't think he'd leave it behind and had to be close by.

'Peter, are you there?' Frobisher called out, faking a friendly voice. 'I've got the woman and I have your gun.'

There was no reply.

Frobisher went to the kitchen door and turned on the light. He looked inside. 'Peter?'

No response.

'Do you know why the Dutchman shot Isaac?' asked Glenda, catching a glimpse of the body on the kitchen floor. She decided she might as well find out all she could while she had the opportunity.

'The paper ran out and Isaac ran out of time,' Frobisher replied curtly.

He crossed to the cellar door, opened it and switched on the light. He registered relief when he saw the boxes piled up at the foot of the steps. Handcuffing Glenda to a stair bannister in the hall, he pocketed his revolver and hurried down the steps, eager to open a box to check the contents. He smiled with satisfaction as he saw the bundles of cash and carried the box up to the hall. He repeated the action with the rest of the boxes until he had them stacked by the front door. Then he freed Glenda from the bannister and snapped the bracelet back on her wrist.

'Back to the car,' he instructed.

As she stumbled across to the car, she looked up the deserted lane. What were the police doing? Where were they?

Frobisher put her in the passenger seat while he busied himself transferring the money to the boot of his car. She noted he wasn't in very good condition, sweating a little more each time he staggered through the gate with another box, and she hoped the exertion might trigger a heart attack. But his life was to have another ending altogether, as evidenced by the figure that appeared in the doorway. The figure was shorter, broader, and uglier than Frobisher.

It was the Dutchman!

She caught her breath and her heart beat thunderously as he approached the car carrying the last box, giving her a smug grin that didn't bode well for her future. He placed the box in the boot with the others and climbed into the driver's seat, producing the car keys. She noticed there was blood on the back of his hand.

'Surprised to see me?' he greeted with a sneer.

'Where's Frobisher?' demanded Glenda, already fearing the worst.

The Dutchman laughed derisively. 'Fond of 'im, are yer?'

'What's happened to him?'

The smile vanished and his eyes were cold and calculating.

'You ask too many questions.'

He started the engine and slipped the car into gear. As they reached the end of Turnpike Lane, Glenda saw a flashing blue light approaching from the right, along the Colchester Road. To avoid the police car, they turned left, picking up speed as they raced along the main road for a short distance before taking a right fork down a narrow track.

'Where does this go?' the Dutchman demanded.

Not wishing to help him, Glenda said

nothing. He stabbed her in the thigh with a hard finger.

'It goes to the lake,' she answered grudgingly, calling up childhood memories as she shifted away from him towards the door.

'And then where?'

She remembered collecting blackberries by the lake shore and watching the huge carp basking in the sun just below the surface, but not much more. She was fairly certain it was a dead end and hoped he would be trapped.

'It goes along by the lake and then across fields I think,' she replied. 'It's a long time since I came down here, so I can't be sure.'

The Dutchman slowed down as the road ahead was barred by a double gate. 'Is this it?'

She nodded. 'Yes, through the gates.'

The Dutchman got out of the car and pulled the gates open. They were old, rickety, and almost falling off their hinges. He drove through the gap, the car headlights fanning out over an expanse of fresh water. He turned sharply left by the lakeside and put his foot down, but the car slewed alarmingly on the muddy surface, creating deep ruts and forcing him to slow right down.

'What's that ahead?' he demanded, seeing posts and some sort of structure beyond them.

'It's an old wooden bridge,' she answered.

It spanned a narrow waterway that fed into the lake; meant for horse and cart traffic, it was now partially rotten. The car was halfway across when its weight proved too much for the old bridge. With an ominous creaking, the supports beneath the wheels began to shift sideways.

There was a sharp crack as the timbers gave way.

The car lurched alarmingly, throwing them both forwards, their heads hitting the windscreen.

The collapse was very quick, like an earthquake tremor. The car was tipped forward precariously at a dangerous angle, propped up against a post that was obviously rotten through, and the only thing stopping them from pitching into the lake. They both sat very still, staring out of the windscreen at the stretch of water before them. The Dutchman's face was contorted with rage. He slammed his hand against the steering wheel with a string of oaths and turned the engine off.

'I've got to get out of the car,' Glenda said, panicking. 'Take these cuffs off me. It could go at any moment.'

The Dutchman turned on her angrily, his scar livid, his face a mask of fury. 'You're going nowhere,' he snarled. 'I've got a special plan for you.'

11

Mr. Budd arrived at Well End twenty minutes after leaving Shinglesea Landing stage. A local constable was standing guard outside the house. A frustrated Detective Inspector Morrison was waiting to meet them. He looked grim and disappointed.

'I got here as soon as I could,' he explained to Mr. Budd. 'The road from Shorewell Island to the mainland was flooded with the high tide and I had trouble getting across. I'm very much afraid we're too late.'

'There's no sign of WPC Lane?' enquired a disgruntled Mr. Budd.

The superintendent was shivering with cold, his face beaten red-raw by the wind and spray. His coat and hat were damp with salt water. Standing next to him, Sergeant Leek looked the epitome of misery, his hair plastered to the top of his head, his face long and sallow.

'I'm afraid not, sir,' answered Morrison. He jerked his head towards the house. 'There are two dead bodies inside, one in the hall and the other in the kitchen. Apart from them, we've seen no sign of anyone. We've searched the house and the barn.' He looked shaken. 'We're not used to this sort of thing around here.'

'I'd better take a look,' said Mr. Budd, entering the house.

When the superintendent reached the kitchen, he paused just inside, rubbing his chin as he looked down at the man lying on the kitchen floor. He bent forward and examined the dead man's features, remembering the photograph he'd seen recently at Joseph Fisk's house in Chiswick.

'Do you know this man?' asked Morrison, seeing the look of recognition on Mr. Budd's face.

'I've never met 'im before, but unless I'm very much mistaken, his name's Isaac Fisk. He's a genius at engraving counterfeit plates and a survivor of the German concentration camps.'

Mr. Budd moved over to the stove and held out his hands to warm them while slowly shaking his head.

'After all he must 'ave been through, it's a sad way to end a life,' he remarked. 'We found his brother Joseph earlier, shot dead in the vault of his bank. It's been a busy night, Inspector.' He stifled a yawn. 'Where's the other body?'

'In the cellar, sir,' answered Morrison, stepping into the hall. 'It's this way.'

Mr. Budd stood at the entrance to the cellar, quickly taking in the scene before him. He noted the printing press and the counterfeiting equipment, but the focus of his attention was the body that lay at the bottom of the cellar steps in a pool of blood. He recognised the prone figure immediately.

'Frobisher,' he said to Leek.

'What's he doing here?' asked the sergeant.

'It's that chap from the Bank of England!' exclaimed Bentley, looking over the detective's shoulder,

'The very same,' answered Mr. Budd. 'His expertise was banknotes, and he can't be accused of deviatin' from that pursuit. Temptation proved too much for 'im. These criminals are like maggots in a barrel,' he murmured. 'They eat each other up until you end up with one big maggot.' He backed away from the cellar entrance. 'You said there was a pile of cash at the bottom of these steps?' he asked Bentley.

'That's what WPC Lane told me, sir,' Bentley confirmed.

'It's obviously not 'ere now,' said the detective, his eyes narrowing as he stared at the empty space where the money should have been.

'Do you have any idea who's responsible, sir?' asked Inspector Morrison.

'I 'ave a very good idea,' answered Mr. Budd, stifling a yawn. 'A very dangerous individual with a scar down one side of 'is face who goes by the name of Peter Van der Horst. I strongly suspect he's taken this money WPC Lane told you about. Most likely 'e's taken WPC Lane as well, most certainly against her will, because it doesn't look like 'e's under arrest, does it? I suspect 'e's taken her as a hostage.

We've no time to lose.'

'Unless she managed to escape,' Bentley suggested hopefully.

'We don't know what 'appened here,' said the big man. 'I'm assumin' the Dutchman got free and killed Frobisher. He can't 'ave been gone for long. We must 'ave just missed 'im.

Bentley knew Glenda had an automatic. What if she'd shot Frobisher? What if it was the other way around, and the Dutchman hadn't got free but was still her prisoner? He didn't say anything in case he got her into trouble.

'I think if she 'ad escaped, she wouldn't 'ave gone far,' Mr. Budd said. 'She'd 'ave showed up by now, seeing the police presence.'

'I've set road blocks on the Colchester Road and the road into Marshford,' Morrison confirmed. 'We've blocked the only two roads that lead anywhere. Apart from them, there's a dead-end track that leads nowhere.'

'It must lead somewhere,' replied Mr. Budd irritably.

'Turner Lake,' answered the inspector

promptly. 'It's a large expanse of water.'

Mr. Budd thought for a moment before reaching a decisive plan of action. With surprising agility, he climbed the cellar steps.

'May we take your car, Morrison?' he requested urgently over his shoulder, addressing the inspector. 'I've a strong feelin' this 'track to nowhere' has to be the one we're lookin' for.'

Morrison jumped in the front of the police car with Joe Bentley at the wheel, while Mr. Budd clambered into the back followed by Sergeant Leek. The hapless sergeant had barely got the passenger door closed before the car surged forward, with an explosion of dirt from the rear wheels as Bentley put his foot down.

'Turn left onto the Colchester road,' Morrison instructed Bentley as they came to the end of Turnpike Lane. 'Now, we go along this main road for a short while . . . '

Morrison kept his eyes peeled until he saw the opening up ahead. 'You see that turning off to the right?'

'Of course I can see it,' replied Bentley impatiently, forgetting he was talking to a superior.

'That goes to the lake,' Morrison said, with a sharp look as Bentley changed gear and swerved onto the narrow track in a cloud of dust.

Low hedges that at first hemmed them in soon gave way to a grassy marshland, revealing the flat desolate landscape upon either side of the road. They came to open gates and saw before them a wide stretch of water reflecting the early light. Bentley drove through the gate, unable to avoid the fresh muddy wheel tracks.

'There's a vehicle been here recently,' he said, skidding sharp left to follow the lakeside.

About halfway along the shore, a football pitch away, they could see a car — but something was wrong. The car wasn't moving, and was in a precarious position, tipped forward at a steep angle. All eyes were focused upon the stationary vehicle.

'There are two people still in the car,

sir,' Bentley said, peering through the windscreen.

As he approached Frobisher's car, Bentley recognised Glenda in the passenger seat. The driver had to be the Dutchman.

'They're obviously stranded,' commented Morrison. 'The bridge has collapsed!'

Mr. Budd removed a snub-nosed revolver from his coat pocket and rested it on his lap.

The Dutchman wound down his window. He put his hand up as a *stop* gesture, and threatened them with the automatic that he had retrieved from Frobisher's coat pocket.

'Stop at once or I shoot the girl!'

'Do as he says,' Mr. Budd instructed.

Bentley braked hard and eased his door open less than an inch. He took his hands off the wheel poised ready for action. His body was taut like a coiled spring.

'Nobody do anything 'asty. Leave this to me,' warned Mr. Budd.

He heaved his bulk out of the police car and, keeping his revolver hidden, took a few steps towards the stranded vehicle.

'Be reasonable, Van der Horst,' he addressed the Dutchman. 'We don't want any more deaths. Give this up now.'

Van der Horst was at his most dangerous and unpredictable, and had the look of a trapped animal. 'All of you get out of the car or I shoot the girl,' he threatened.

Nobody moved.

Losing his patience, the Dutchman waved the gun at them as proof of his intention.

Mr. Budd gave a slight nod to the occupants of the police car. One by one they complied, until they were all standing on the grass. It was clear the Dutchman had no qualms about using Glenda as a hostage to achieve what he wanted. Mr. Budd knew that meant commandeering the police car as his only hope of getting away. A police vehicle and an automatic pistol might just give him a chance at the road blocks.

'Step over there,' the Dutchman commanded, waving his automatic towards a mass of dead bramble bushes some fifty yards away. 'Step over there now or I shoot her in the leg.'

This threat sounded much worse than his threat to kill her, which would have left him with no protection. His threat worked, because no one doubted from the tone of his voice that he would carry it out. Without further discussion, the group began trudging through foot-high grass towards the brambles.

'What can we do, sir?' Bentley asked Mr. Budd, beside himself with worry.

'We let him take the police car and we wait for another opportunity to rescue WPC Lane,' said Mr. Budd sympathetically. 'What we mustn't do is escalate this situation to a bad outcome.'

The small group were halfway towards the dead brambles when the Dutchman kicked open the door of the car. He attempted to step out, but the sudden shift of weight was all that was needed for the fragile supports to give way. With a sharp splintering of rotten timbers, the car was propelled forward.

The moment he realised what had happened Bentley ran like a hare, sprinting towards the bridge.

The Dutchman lost his balance, throwing up his hands as the bonnet hit the surface with a huge splash. The force of the water pushed him back inside the car as it burst through the opening.

Glenda had sat listening to the exchanges between the Dutchman and Mr. Budd, dreading what might happen next. Handcuffed, she was helpless to take part in preventing the Dutchman from trying to escape. She realised her fate was in the hands of whoever won through.

Now, thrown forward in her seat, her eyes opened wide with horror as her head hit the windscreen again just before the car lurched into the lake. The water leapt towards her. It was freezing cold as it smacked into her and began swirling around her legs, rising quickly up to her waist and then her chin. The car was filling up so rapidly she had only time for one final breath before she went under.

As Bentley reached the shoreline, panting and gasping for air after his sprint, only the boot of the car was visible. And then, with a burst of bubbles, it slipped under the surface.

Ice-cold water drove the breath from Bentley's body as he dived without hesitation into the lake. He strained to catch a glimpse of the sinking car, but due to the churned-up murky water, he couldn't see it until he physically bumped into it. He groped for a door handle and pulled for all he was worth. The door opened, releasing a stream of bubbles as Glenda let some air out of her lungs. He grabbed at her coat and tugged her out of the car. Kicking back against the bodywork, he managed to propel them both upwards just before the car slid off a narrow ledge it was resting on, with the Dutchman struggling inside.

Kicking down against the water with all his strength, Bentley propelled them both upwards until he broke the surface. They both gulped in lungfuls of air.

Morrison had already taken a rope from the boot of the police car. The moment the two of them broke the surface, he threw them a line that was sufficient for Bentley to grab hold of.

Morrison pulled them out.

They both laid Glenda gently on her stomach to cough up any water she'd ingested. Morrison unlocked the handcuffs and gently rested her arms by her side.

Bentley was preparing to dive in again, in an attempt to rescue the Dutchman, when Mr. Budd grabbed his arm and held him back.

'It's not worth the risk, lad. Save the hangman some rope.'

★ ★ ★

The Dutchman had proved he was very efficient at getting rid of people when it suited him. Ironically, through his own carelessness, he had got rid of himself. His body, trapped by his coat, was recovered by divers from the wreckage of the car lying thirty feet down on the bed of Turner Lake. In the car boot was found a fortune in soggy banknotes.

Mr. Budd sat in his dingy office at Scotland Yard and lit a black cigar. He blew out a cloud of smoke, and with an expression of satisfaction watched it unfurl in the air as it dissipated. He was reviewing the fruits of his enquiries regarding the counterfeit case prior to a meeting with the assistant commissioner, Colonel Blair.

The report on the fingerprints taken from the shed at Paradise Street, and from the *Black Rose*, recovered from Bow Creek, matched those of a Gerhard Schuster, alias Peter Van der Horst. Mr. Budd remembered the words of Mrs. Olive Samuels telling him that Isaac Fisk lived in Amsterdam, in Van der Hoopstraat, with her brother, and that Olive and Corinna were German Jews originally from Danzig with the surname of Schuster.

Further reports from Interpol enabled Mr. Budd to piece together why Mrs. Samuels hadn't gone into further detail about the man who was her and Corrina's brother. If she knew anything of his history, she'd probably want to forget they were related. Was she entirely innocent? He pondered this question as he enjoyed his cigar.

Gerhard Schuster had been the black sheep of the family, a career criminal known to the Dutch authorities who'd used several other aliases. He'd served four years in a Dutch prison for causing grievous bodily harm and two years for selling fake passports. When Isaac had come to live in Van der Hoopstraat after the war, Schuster seized an opportunity to put him to work forging passports, ration coupons and other documents — anything people would pay to have faked.

Another Interpol report concerned the German paper manufacturer Dieter Kretschmann, from whom Peter Van der Horst had procured the special paper on which to print the counterfeit banknotes. Eight months ago, Kretschmann's body had been found floating in the Amstel. He had died due to a severe blow to his head, not unlike that suffered by Derek Lane. The Dutch police were maintaining an open file on his death.

Mr. Budd threw down the report. He was sure Kretschmann's death was an attempt by the Dutchman to cover his tracks and that he had cold-bloodedly murdered him as he had murdered Joseph and Isaac Fisk, and no doubt murdered Percival Silk, whose body, reduced to ashes, had never been recovered.

The autopsy on Detective Inspector Derek Lane had showed algae had been found in the lungs and the stomach but had not been found in the liver or kidneys, proving that his heart had not been beating when he entered the water. The evidence pointed to a suspicious death.

Mr. Budd surmised that, under the directions of Frobisher, Derek Lane had been lured to Mews Street, where he'd been struck on the head with sufficient force to kill him. The platinum-blonde mannequin, V7, had been deliberately stuffed full of counterfeit banknotes and placed in the rowing boat with the detective's body. The Dutchman had drifted the rowing boat into the path of the duty boat, knowing at that time of the morning there would be little other traffic on the river to get in the way. The counterfeiters wanted the mannequin discovered and Derek Lane eliminated. They were deliberately laying a false trail all the way back to Amsterdam, when all the time they were holed up in Essex.

Derek Lane was gone but not forgotten. There was a lengthy funeral procession, with a full police escort, for the officer murdered in the line of duty. Glenda felt very proud that day.

Fisk and Fossett closed down. Everyone who worked for the bank lost their jobs. The bank was declared insolvent once the illegal assets were removed. It would be a very long time before the City of London Police managed to separate the genuine assets of the bank from those that were illegal, and it would take even longer for the counterfeit notes to be completely removed from circulation.

Mr. Budd didn't like to dwell on what might have happened to Glenda if Joe Bentley hadn't been quick to rescue her. Despite being nearly murdered and scared out of her wits, she had come through her experience relatively unscathed. She had lost her mother in the Blitz and her father in the line of duty but she wouldn't be left alone.

A few weeks after her father's funeral, Mr. Budd received an invitation to an engagement party that was to take place in the second week of May. It was to be held on a river cruiser.

He smiled as he took a long draw on his cigar. Joe and Glenda deserved to be happy.

GRIM DEATH
MURDER IN MANUSCRIPT
THE GLASS ARROW
THE THIRD KEY
THE ROYAL FLUSH MURDERS
THE SQUEALER
MR. WHIPPLE EXPLAINS
THE SEVEN CLUES
THE CHAINED MAN
THE HOUSE OF THE GOAT
THE FOOTBALL POOL MURDERS
THE HAND OF FEAR
SORCERER'S HOUSE
THE HANGMAN
THE CON MAN
MISTER BIG
THE JOCKEY
THE SILVER HORSESHOE
THE TUDOR GARDEN MYSTERY
THE SHOW MUST GO ON
SINISTER HOUSE
THE WITCHES' MOON
ALIAS THE GHOST
THE LADY OF DOOM
THE BLACK HUNCHBACK

We do hope that you have enjoyed reading this large print book.

Did you know that all of our titles are available for purchase?

We publish a wide range of high quality large print books including:
Romances, Mysteries, Classics
General Fiction
Non Fiction and Westerns

Special interest titles available in large print are:
The Little Oxford Dictionary
Music Book, Song Book
Hymn Book, Service Book

Also available from us courtesy of Oxford University Press:
Young Readers' Dictionary
(large print edition)
Young Readers' Thesaurus
(large print edition)

For further information or a free brochure, please contact us at:
Ulverscroft Large Print Books Ltd.,
The Green, Bradgate Road, Anstey,
Leicester, LE7 7FU, England.
Tel: (00 44) **0116 236 4325**
Fax: (00 44) **0116 234 0205**

MYSTERY OF THE RUBY

V. J. Banis

According to legend, the Baghdad ruby has the power to grant anything the heart desires. But a curse lies upon it, and all who own the stone are destined to die tragically, damned for eternity. When Joseph Hanson inherits the gem after his uncle's bizarre murder, his wife Liza is afraid. Though his fortune grows, he becomes surly and brutal. And suddenly Liza knows there's only one way to stave off the curse of centuries — she must sacrifice her own soul to save the man she loves.

LONELY BUSINESS

Steven Fox

Herbie Vore, mystery writer and recent widower, leads a lonely, uneventful existence — until he begins to receive threatening postcards and packages referring to Cindy, his crush from long ago. When a teenager arrives at his door claiming to be the son of his old flame, Herbie learns that Cindy has also been receiving mysterious notes and phone calls. Who could want to harm them after all these years — and why? The investigation will uncover more than Herbie ever imagined — and possibly cost him his life . . .

TREACHERY IN THE WILDERNESS

Victor Rousseau

Joe Bostock and his chief engineer Will Carruthers are engaged on building a railway line in the wilds of Manitoba that will open up rich wheat lands for settlers — but the Big Muskeg swamp seems likely to ruin the construction scheme. When an unseen assailant treacherously picks Joe off with a rifle, Will, although wounded himself, vows to complete the railroad and bring his friend's murderer to justice. But he is hampered and his life threatened at every turn by a crooked syndicate led by a rival contractor . . .

MR. MIDNIGHT

Gerald Verner

Gordan Cross, crime reporter for the *Daily Clarion*, is detailed to discover the identity of a man known as Mr. Midnight, the mastermind behind a series of robberies and murders. Acting on a tip, he investigates The Yellow Orchid nightclub — and meets a variety of odd and suspicious people, including two who quickly turn up dead. How is the classy club implicated in the Midnight business — and who is the mysterious informant, 'A. Smith'? Teamed with Superintendent Budd of Scotland Yard, Gordan is determined to uncover the truth.

HAUNTED HELEN

V. J. Banis

Mentally scarred by her parents' violent deaths, Helen Sparrow was sent for treatment at a residential psychiatric clinic. Now discharged, she returns to a shadowy old mansion, the scene of both the murders and her repressed, unhappy childhood. But she senses an evil presence in the house: something that follows her along the gloomy halls and whispers just on the edge of her consciousness. Is she insane? Or does some supernatural echo of that terrible night lurk within those walls?

SAY IT WITH BULLETS

Arlette Lees

Two abused and neglected children find sanctuary with a neighboring rancher. Out West, a gold prospector's widow must evade the clutches of a corrupt sheriff. Defying doctor's orders, a wounded cop searches for his missing rebellious sister. After fleeing Hitler's Berlin, a Jewish father and daughter will find unexpected danger in California. A girl's dowdy stepmother is hiding a dangerous secret. And in the gritty underbelly of professional boxing lurks a bloody mystery whose reverberations will echo down several decades.